THE AIRMAN'S DAUGHTER

THE AIRMAN'S DAUGHTER

Antony Day
□

ISBN: 9798394581823

Imprint: Independently published

Cover design by: Martin Lore

For my Mother

Chapter 1

Anna and the Ghost

London, November 1989

She had an overwhelming sense that she was being watched. Anna looked up from her copy of Crime and Punishment and scanned the bar. It was empty. Even the barman had disappeared somewhere. Outside, a lone figure strutted past, making their way along Marchmont Street, the shallow sun lighting up their back as they left her frame of view. The feeling passed, she lit a cigarette and returned to her book.

Vigilance had become a state of being for Anna, but she kept scolding herself for being paranoid. London gave her anonymity, and was far enough removed from her previous life to allow her to feel comfortable to come into bars on her own, sit on a stool and while away some time. She might catch up on her reading or sketch out the idea for a poem or song lyric. The pub opening hours were one positive change she had returned to. Not quite the continental laissez-faire that she was used to, but at least they didn't throw you out in the afternoon. But the change had been recent, and it seemed Londoners had not really got to grips with these European customs. So in some pubs, like this one on the edge of Bloomsbury, she pretty much had the place to herself.

She would have to get to work in an hour, but for Anna this was good re-charge time. She was lonely, alone, actually done in. She felt abandoned and exhausted - even though she knew she had done most of the running away, and more than once. A serial absconder was how she sometimes thought of herself. She felt time passing and opportunities slipping away, although these afternoons didn't feel like wasted time. They gave her a sense of being able to embed herself back into her old community. She desperately needed to rebuild.

Since she had arrived back in London three months earlier she had achieved three things: separation from her life in Berlin, enough work to get by, and a small network of acquaintances, some picked up from her earlier life in the city. Many of her old crowd had moved on, and she had cut them off completely when she moved. She would not class any of the people she hung out with now as close friends, and she was not able to share her story with them. Not yet. Maybe never. She was an enigma. She had no intention of going back to Berlin, and had resolved to carve out a new life, even though she had no idea what might come next. But she had to admit in her lowest moments that her existence felt ephemeral and transient. There was a big hole in her life.

She was fully absorbed in her book, trying to draw parallels between nineteenth century St Petersburg and twentieth century Berlin, and recognising people she knew in the tortured and compromised souls of Dostoevsky's imagination. Perhaps some light shifted, a door was opened, or a chair scraped on the floor, but reflecting afterwards she could not recall any warning. So what happened next was a surprise.

'Is this what we were all fighting for?' said a voice, that suddenly burst into her world of silent concentration.

She bolted upright, giving a little gasp. In front of her, a few yards down the bar, stood a man, she guessed in his sixties or early seventies. He was leaning over the newspaper on the bar, which had a large picture of people climbing on a wall, with the headline: Together At Last.

'So they opened the border?' he said, looking up at her.

"Jesus you gave me a start. Where did you come from?'

'What do you think it all means? Is it a good thing?'

'I've no idea, I haven't really given it much thought'

Of course this wasn't true, she'd seen the TV news the night before. People flooding through the checkpoint gates into West Berlin, or dancing on top of the wall. A wall that had been a backdrop to her life these past few years, a symbol, an obstacle, an ever-present shadow. Staring at the TV pictures she almost believed she was there among the crowds. Her former adoptive home now being transformed in ways she couldn't begin to understand. Right now she was confused, and a little stunned, with a jumble of thoughts. This man spoke as if he walked right out of Brief Encounter. She hadn't heard the door, no footsteps, and she'd only just checked to see she was alone.

'Don't you think you should?' he said.

'It's not my problem. I've got my own life to worry about.'

'Isn't this important enough? Don't you have friends there?'

'You ask a lot of questions. I don't know you...'

'But I know you.'

"Oh, this is weird. I've got to go' She started putting her book and cigarettes into her bag.

'I'm sorry, I really don't mean to alarm you. But you see I have been looking for you for a long time, and I really would like a chat.'

'That's it, I'm out of here.' She hopped off the stool, slung her bag onto her shoulder and picked up her leather jacket. She made to give him a wide berth.

'Please. Please don't leave. I didn't mean to alarm you. I know who you are, Anna, and I really do need to talk with you.'

She stopped and turned as she came level with him. 'Who are you? What do you want?'

She glanced at the exit, checked behind her for a route out the back. She was wired for flight but rooted out of curiosity. She looked at him properly for the first time. He was older than she first thought. He stood tall and straight, with laughter wrinkles at the edges of his eyes, grey hair combed straight back, slightly curled behind the ears. Beard and moustache neatly trimmed, a well-tailored overcoat with a felt collar. Too old for a policeman, she thought. Smartly dressed, very London establishment – so he was unlikely to have followed her from Berlin. A private investigator perhaps? She decided to go along with this assumption.

'I don't know how you found me, but you can tell her I'm fine, and to stop stalking me.'

'Who?'

'My mother.'

'Oh she didn't send me. But it does concern her, and your father. And it feels very important that I share it with you.'

While she glared, he continued to look at her, mildly inquisitive, the corners of his mouth and creases at his eyes indicating a faint amusement. He didn't look threatening, but she was wary all the same. She got the sense that he was looking deep into her, searching for something. She started to wonder if she had seen him somewhere before. He seemed vaguely familiar.

'You were very easy to find you know. Finally, anyway.' He chuckled a little. He seemed to have a sense of his own humour. She said nothing and edged around him further.

'Look, I'm actually as surprised to see you. I hadn't planned this. But since I've found you there are a few things you need to know,' he paused. 'You might just need to be prepared.'

'Prepared for what?'

'That depends quite a lot on you.'

He was making her more nervous now, but she had to hear more. If he was connected to people in Germany then this could be very bad for her. But he had mentioned her parents, so maybe this was something altogether different, but deeply unsettling nevertheless. These types of conversations never happened outside of films and TV dramas. Whatever it was, then, wasn't normal, and avoiding it might be a mistake.

'Let's find a quiet corner,' he said, looking around the deserted pub. The barman reappeared and the stranger said, 'can you do me a coffee?'

'Coffee? Mate, this is a pub. Where are you from?' He sounded antipodean.

'Don't worry, I'll just have water. What would you like Anna?'

'No, nothing.' She wanted to get on with this. Get it over with.

'First,' she said when they had sat down, 'tell me exactly who you are and how you know me. And my mother.'

'I'll come to all of that. But first I want to take you through a few facts about yourself. Get a bit of context.'

'Who ARE you?' she demanded.

'For now, Anna, just think of me as a ghost.'

***

Anna walked out into the twilight an hour later, vaguely conscious that she was going to be late for work, but more aware of her heightened anxiety. If everything she had heard were true then she was going to have to re-appraise her whole life.

As she crossed Leigh Street she glanced to her left down the curve of Cartwright Gardens, at the exact spot where she had first met Aaron eight years earlier. She pictured herself walking towards the corner of Burton Place on her way to see her best friend Molly, head full of a new song she wanted the band to try out. Molly and Aaron almost bumping into her as they turned the corner. Even now she could still feel that shock of seeing him for the first time. Dyed black hair with a fringe that flopped over even darker eyes; clothes part punk, part rockabilly, and an air of aloofness. Molly hadn't mentioned him before, so this looked like a fresh acquisition. That hadn't bothered Anna – he looked dangerous to know, and she was immediately drawn to him. They were all playing at being dangerous to know, her King's Cross group of punks and misfits. Some of them actually were dangerous, and the excitement was not quite knowing who was for real, and who was pretending. It was a fun way to be, until people got hurt. The man given a restraining order after drunkenly throwing his girlfriend down the tenement stairwell; the arson attack on the (thankfully empty) flat of a bass player she vaguely knew; the drug gang fights in the courtyards. There were other stories, she later assumed to be apocryphal, of chainsaw attacks, cheaply cut drugs, band gear stolen at knifepoint after a gig, that all added to the allure. Meanwhile the real underworld culture of King's Cross went on around them, oblivious to their imaginings, and getting on with the serious business of carving out a living in the city. These worlds sometimes clashed when a small-time criminal would break into a flat and steal instruments (usually the only valuables around), and fence them out to Birmingham or Glasgow. The seasoned local operators would get annoyed at this, apologise to the victim on behalf of the 'honest crooks of the Cross' that these boys will be taught not to 'shit in their own back yard'. It was bad for business to steal from your neighbours, brought the police crawling around where they were not needed. Aaron, as she was to learn, blurred the lines between these two worlds, and his ambiguity would captivate her and almost destroy her.

How on earth had this 'ghost' known about Aaron, and her subsequent odyssey to fix his life? She had told no-one his story, and had simply upped and left on a whim, following him back to Hamburg. No forwarding address, no letters home to say where she was going, all contact cut. No-one could know any of it. She wondered whether she might have been spied on, and that police intelligence had been better than she thought. But if that were the case why had she not been detained – or at least questioned? Her introduction to the underworld in Germany had been as shocking as it was instructive, and while she had been peripheral, she knew things. And yet no police, no investigators, or anyone else (people she really worried about) for that matter, had bothered her. She had felt immune and alive in her world on the edge. Was it really all some sort of smokescreen, a game of pretend? She had occasionally wondered whether Aaron ever told her a single true word. Now she was questioning it all over again. Her 'ghost' had brought all that doubt back. He seemed to know her movements of the past eight years – the major events at least, when she was convinced that they were unknowable.

But then he had gone back further, and had told her things, and questioned things, about her parents that she wasn't ready to process. She was too intent on piecing her present self back together. She now felt fully deconstructed. Her past was going to have to wait a while.

She arrived at work half an hour late. Her pager had been going off all the way to the hospital.

'Where the hell have you been? We've got a job to do.' Bert the chargehand was generally a genial sort, but could get grumpy under pressure. These evening shifts especially pissed him off, depriving him of a night in the pub. 'I know you've got a degree and all, but it doesn't mean you can waltz in anytime you like. If the operating theatres aren't able to open on time tomorrow morning we'll be in deep shit. And you'll be looking for a new contract.'

She didn't mind the ear-bashing from Bert so much. She was a woman in a man's world, and he was a black man in a predominantly white man's world – they each recognised in the other the constant subliminal work-place discrimination that they experienced, and tended to look out for each other. It was Mo she had a problem with – all pally-pally with his deep sexist undertones, she was sure he was a racist too. Here he came now to back up his mate. 'Where have you been?' he echoed, 'we've got a job to do.' Technically she was their boss tonight, but (a) she was on a temporary contract, and (b) she was a woman. Never mind that she was a qualified engineer. In Germany she would have had status. Here she had to negotiate for every bit of recognition. She mumbled something about how they could've got started without her and headed off to pick up her equipment. What she really wanted to do was make a phone call, but it was going to have to wait. The theatre air-conditioning was the priority for now, and she had measurements to take, and Bert and Mo to placate.

Later that evening, during a break, a thought struck her. Something had been churning away inside, and she realised this was beginning to get to her. The three engineers were having a fag when she blurted out –

'Here, Bert - how do you find out about what happened to people in the war?'

'I dunno. Never thought about it. I guess you could start with the Imperial War Museum. I'll bet they have loads of records. Why?'

'Oh, nothing. Just something I heard today. Made me curious.'

Her pager went off, so she found a phone and called the operator. 'Is that Anna Highcroft? There's a call for you.'

☐

Chapter 2

Losing his wings

April 1943

Flight Lieutenant Douglas Highcroft sat in the squadron leader's office at RAF Scorton waiting for his commanding officer to arrive. There was no room to sit in the cramped outer office, and the adjutant had nodded him through. It seemed to Doug that everyone on the base now gave him a knowing look that said he probably needed to sit down. His hip was in fact giving him some gyp today, and despite his restlessness and slight anxiety he nevertheless took up the offer.

Outside and overhead a group of three returning Beaufighters were circling the field to land on the easterly runway, and he felt that small pang of jealousy that rose in him every time there was a successful return. They had been on an early morning patrol, but he hadn't heard reports of any incidents overnight. He had loved flying, and he was desperate to get back to it. The war was now passing him by, and he felt he had let the squadron down by getting injured. So now perhaps was the news he had been waiting for.

Squadron Leader Alderton arrived, and much to Doug's surprise he was accompanied by the Wing Commander.

'Ahh, Highgate' said the wing commander

'Highcroft, sir'

'What? Oh yes, sorry - associations and all that.' The wing commander was from Hampstead and had been racked with homesickness all through this blessed war. He adopted a constant lens of a view of St Paul's in all his dealings with people. 'You a Londoner?'

'No sir, Torbay actually'

'Hmm Devon. Went there once. Family there?'

'Only my mother sir.'

The commanding officer seemed to drift off into his own train of thought.

'So Highcroft,' said the squadron leader 'you've abandoned your stick today I see. Your medical report is very positive. Good progress.'

'Yes sir, all fixed up now. Raring to get back to flying duties. And keen to get back to where I can be of most use again, sir.'

Doug had been placed in charge of a ground radar operations team. He had shown a strong grasp of the technology during his training, which was why he had been assigned to 219 Beaufighter night flight squadron. Following his injury it seemed natural to get him to develop the skills of the ground crews. Their role was becoming increasingly critical.

'Yes, Flight Lieutenant, that's what we wanted to talk to you about' said the wing commander. 'Big developments under way, with some major reorganisations.' He looked directly at the young grounded flying officer with his chin tucked in, his eyes peering through his bushy eyebrows, 'New orders for 219 Squadron just in, which will be heading out to North Africa. The flights will be distributed to give night-time cover on the defensive positions.'

'North Africa. My brother's out there, sir. He's a captain in the Royal Artillery. When's the move planned for, sir?'

'Very soon' said the squadron leader, and after a short pause, 'so while you are making great progress, it doesn't look as if you're going to be fit enough to come with us. You won't be seeing your brother for a while yet.'

'You're being reassigned' said the senior officer, 'to ground-controlled interception. Your radar experience is going to be vital to the war effort.'

This was the worst possible news for the 25-year-old airman. He'd signed up with the specific intent to fly, to stand on the shoulders of the Battle of Britain heroes. Doug felt that he must have looked deflated. His shoulders dropped, and somehow his expression lost its usual air of optimism and bravura. He said nothing.

'Look, Highcroft', said the squadron leader, 'you really are not able to pilot a Beau right now, and we need to put you somewhere you can make a solid contribution.'

'Where would that be?'

'GCI Staythorpe, it's a new mobile radar station set up near Nottingham. Needs the latest equipment to be commissioned. It's the future of successful forward combat.'

He was dimly aware of the recently landed Beaufighter engines winding down. The buzz of his expectations were similarly waning. Bloody hell, he thought, they might as well send me over to the army. He realised the squadron leader was still speaking.

'We need good officers to keep up morale on the ground. You can be a bit casual for my liking, but the men like you. They trust you. Radar is going to make all the difference, and you'll be right in the metaphorical thick of it.'

When Doug stepped out into the daylight he became keenly aware of his surroundings. It was a bright spring morning, with the green grass across the airfield outshining the grey render of the drab single-storey building behind him. Overhead, an ash tree still in the throes of unfurling its summer foliage. Against this backdrop his mood had now plummeted to a new low he had never felt before. Even when he was stretchered from his plane after the shrapnel had torn into his upper thigh in that tussle with a couple of Junker 88s, even then he knew he would get himself fixed up and return to the air. It's what airmen did. They died, or kept trying. His recovery had been frustratingly slow, and he hated hobbling into the Ops room in the morning to motivate the crew to run the equipment checks one more time. But he always knew he'd get back in a plane. And now - GCI - and where the hell was Staythorpe? What could possibly be good about bloody Staythorpe?

Well, he thought, if I'm going to be miserable I might as well share it with the crew, let's have a party. Doug was known for his parties. Whether it was a few rounds of drinks at the local pub, or some ad hoc gathering in the officers' mess, Doug always had a knack of turning it into an occasion. His quick-fire wit, the extra gin conjured from somewhere, the urgency of making the most of this unnatural throwing together of disparate characters, were Doug's way of getting through this war. He had volunteered for the RAF in 1940 during the heat of the Battle of Britain, convinced he would become a Spitfire pilot, but by the time he had finished his operational training the battle was long won and Fighter Command had new priorities. He was transferred into Coastal Command, and soon started to pilot the long-range Beaufighter on patrols over the Norwegian coast. Outwardly he appeared a natural pilot, a team player, the positive spirit in the crew, but inside it kept gnawing away that the war was draining his opportunities. Some undefined void sat in him - a longing for a purpose. His fellow aircrew seemed to thrive on the war, it was their purpose. So he threw himself into the mix and, being a sociable person, determined to have as many good memories of this war as he could. Sometimes the party spirit wiped his memory, but he was pretty sure he was enjoying himself.

He found himself wandering into the crew room. He hadn't quite known where he was heading, he knew he needed to get back to the control room, but this was good enough for now. 'Hello, Duggie, how was your skirmish with the skipper?' It was Brindle, another flying officer and a good enough chap, but not exactly a pal. 'I'll tell you all about it in the Farmers Arms later. Seven o'clock? Tell the team, and make sure the ACWs get wind of it.'

***

Doug stepped into his new room in Rollaston village. He had been billeted with the Palings, a couple in their mid-sixties. Mr Paling had worked before the war at the nearby racecourse, which was now housing the temporary mobile radar interception unit. It had been newly established the previous summer as some kind of experiment. Clearly it had been successful as there was now an equipment upgrade scheduled, and Doug was to oversee the installation and set-up, and training of the crew. There were two other officers of his rank also newly transferred in just ahead of him, Jerry Mays and Vince Reedbanks. They were both a year younger than Doug, and had been trained directly into signals. Neither had any flying experience. This gave Doug an advantage as the man who had not only seen live action, but had been blooded and survived. He wasn't one to use his misfortune to gain a sense of superiority over his fellow officers, but he did understand that it helped him in his greatest endeavour – to be liked. His easy manner, frequent joking and desire to start up a conversation with anyone gave him an air of strong self-confidence, the natural person to take command of circumstances. New comrades often looked to him to be the catalyst for their new bonds.

This did not always give the desired results, however, and in this case there was a sense of unease, especially emanating from Reedbanks. 'You must be Highcroft,' Reedbanks had said when he walked into the crew room for the first time, 'down from 219 I hear'.

'Yes, that's right. Call me Doug. Good to meet you both. Hope you can show me the lie of the land.'

'Well, it's flat and remote. Not much around here to get excited about. It'll be a real comedown for you, I'd guess.'

'Oh, I don't know. I'm sure we can find ways to liven things up. Any good pubs nearby?'

Jerry Mays had been leaning back on his chair, smoking his pipe. He dropped forward, the front legs of the chair thumping onto the wooden floor. 'A couple, they seem to have a few community gatherings - the young farmers and all that. Seems to be where the ACWs like to congregate.'

'Well there's a start.' Doug felt his spirits lifting already.

While he found Mays to be cool and a little distant he nevertheless saw in him some solid dependability. A man with an eye on a solution. Reedbanks, on the other hand, seemed to go out of his way to generate a fog of uncertainty, and to load his asides with indecipherable meaning. They would be working different shifts, so on the one hand Doug thought they could avoid any animosity, but on the other there would be little time to work on winning the man round. In any case they would be handing over to each other and Doug did not want any blame culture for mistakes his team might make. Initially they would be firing up the new radar rigs, and he wanted a trouble-free and seamless transition to the new set-up. He made up his mind to work on Reedbanks, and to pay close attention to his quirks and foibles. Despite being grounded in the doldrums of England, he was buggered if some signals man was going to derail his determination. (Determination for what was a little out of focus, but he had it nevertheless).

The first week on the ad hoc base was surprisingly hard work. Trucks were arriving daily with new gear that needed locating, un-crating and assembling. New complexity arose in establishing ways of connecting and disconnecting the kit quickly and accurately. The system was designed to be mobile and ready to move locations at a moment's notice. The men were still unclear about the purpose of this. The other GCI stations were well-established, and while they might be targets for attack, were built to withstand severe bombardment. That and the fact they were hard to spot from the air and were remote from the major airfields. These were the command and control centres for active operations, where fighters were directed to intercept their targets of incoming bombers or fighter support. A mobile unit here, with no obvious German bombing targets this side of Nottingham, seemed to be a little redundant. In the following weeks they would practise and re-practise the set-up routines that they established, each time shaving minutes off the time it took. Technical crews passed through the station, being trained on these new techniques that they were developing. It seemed they were learning to set up similar units around the country. Doug's former wing commander was right, there were some big changes under way, maybe he wouldn't get too bored after all, and after this war was over he might have some skills he could use.

By the end of June he found he'd been working non-stop, with barely time to get to a pub, let alone organise a shindig. He was sorely in need of some socialising, so when word came round about the young farmers' midsummer 'hop' he felt his expectations rising. He wanted to bond better with the crew, to impress on Reedbanks they should be pals, and to meet some of the young WAAF women he'd been watching as they came in and out of the Ops Room. He had spoken to a few of them, but he hadn't spent any time with them. 'Let's get a gang together and head up to the bash in Staythorpe tonight' he said to Jerry Mays. And together they set about recruiting willing subjects.

Chapter 3

Anna and the museum

London, November 1989

The Fitzroy Tavern in Charlotte Street has one of those London pub histories that you never know whether to believe. Frequented by the literati in times gone by, it was also the home of curious traditions. In the 1940s the landlord would parcel up your change, put a dart through it, and throw it at the ceiling. If it stuck, it stayed there. Once a year the money would be recovered and put towards a seaside trip for the local orphans. Pennies from Heaven. Somehow Anna knew this story, but was never sure where she had picked it up.

She pushed through the crowded bar to find her friend sitting in the corner. Two pints in front of her, ready for the reunion.

'Oh my God, Anna! It's really you!'

'Hello, Jane. So good to see you. Where's Molly? Is she coming?'

'She said she'd meet us later in Soho. You're a tough one to track down. How long have you been back?'

Odd, she thought, her friends couldn't find her but perfect strangers could.

'Sorry I hadn't contacted you sooner. It's been mad trying to find work and a place to live. You know how it is.' She lit a cigarette and took a gulp of her beer. 'I found a place down at Gray's Inn - lucky really, but I just asked around the Cross. Like old times.'

'You've changed, Anna. You've grown your hair, and I never knew you were a natural ash. No longer jet black. It always seemed a trade-mark of yours.'

'Well, you know, things change. I guess it just became too much like hard work keeping up the image.'

'I know. But Molly manages it. Still multi-coloured, always changing things around. Hey, those glasses suit you.'

'Oh these. Too many books and late-night studying wrecked my eyes.'

'But you're still all in black I see – I like the boots! What are you doing for work?'

'Oh, agency stuff. I'm a qualified engineer now. Did some studying in Germany. I'm doing quite a lot of work at UCH at the moment. It pays the bills.'

'Tell me all about Germany! What was it like in Berlin? What happened to Aaron?''

One reason for not seeking out her old friends was because she didn't want to get into all this. She hadn't yet worked out what she wanted to tell people. She deflected as best she could with a drip-feed of information, interspersed with questions about her friend's own life. In this way she managed to disclose the barest amounts of information: she followed Aaron to Germany because she realised he needed help; she needed something to do when she got there so she went to college; Aaron and she had split up about five years ago; she stayed on because she had a job, friends, something of a life in a cool scene. What she didn't say was that Aaron had ended up in prison, and that for her to leave would have felt like betrayal. And that leaving would have drawn attention to herself, which would have been unwise at the time. Perhaps still was.

'So what made you come back?'

'Oh, my mother I guess.' Oh God, where did that come from! 'I thought I needed to see her'. Completely not true.

'How is she?'

'Oh, fine' No idea, actually. What was she doing? Creeping up on her was an understanding that her talk with the 'ghost' had a more destabilising effect than she had thought.

'Actually, Jane, there's something that's really bothering me. About my mother. Well my father. Both of them. I already thought I was a bit fucked up, but now I'm not sure she was entirely honest with me about him.'

'He died when you were little, didn't he?'

'When I was a baby, so she always told me. But now I realise I really don't know what the story was. She never told me anything about him, other than they met in the war, lost touch, and met up again after his first marriage failed. I don't really know how he died - some sort of boating accident she said. So I've been thinking I need to do some research. Find out more about him.'

'Why now? And can't you just ask her?'

'Let's just say a spooky encounter recently made me doubt everything I thought I knew. And in truth I haven't spoken to my mum for some time.' She downed her pint. 'Come on, let's head to the Dog and Duck, I want to get hammered.'

***

'You'll need to book an appointment with the Records Office' the voice said.

'Can you put me through?' Anna asked.

'There's no-one there right now. Can you call back in an hour?'

It was the third time she had called the Imperial War Museum, with the same blank result.

'I just need to find out how I go about getting information on someone's war history'

'Like I said, you need to talk to the Records Office.'

Earlier she had had similar frustrations, first with Somerset House, and then St Catherine's House (where the Somerset people had re-directed her), who seemed to make it incredibly difficult to find out anything about dead people. She had scratched at the surface, only to find no record of her father. True, she had very little to go on. Only her surname - Highcroft; a vague location - South Devon; and a rough date - 1959-60. Her mother had told her so little that she had to guess where they might start searching. Clearly her guesses were rubbish. If only there was a way to speed up these searches – it all took so much time.

So no death certificate. What about birth? Again she had nothing. The new information she had been given didn't help. A rough guess would have put her father's birth year between 1916 to 1922 - given that he'd been a serving officer in the war. A number of Highcrofts were born around that time, right across the country. One in Dorset. But it didn't tell her anything. She could hardly confront her mother - 'Hey, Mum, you've been lying to me. And to prove it I have absolutely no evidence! What do you have to say to that?'. She was going to need more.

She kept doubting whether she needed to confront her mother, or whether she just didn't want to. They had exchanged a few letters while she was in Germany, but she wanted to keep the contact to a minimum. She couldn't reveal the trouble she thought she was in. And while her mother would have been worried sick, Anna had walled off her life from everybody. Now that she was back in England she felt guilty that she had still not made contact. The need to explain herself, her actions, her life, held her back. And now she would have to restart their relationship with a row, more than likely, having the growing feeling that she knew nothing about who her mother really was. She wondered whether anyone knew anything about their parents - where they came from, what life experiences shaped them. Did children ever stop to consider that their parents were in fact sentient and emotional beings?

All that Anna had known about her mother's past was the story she had been told several times. Always the same set of events, in the same order, with the same level of detail. There were never any other little anecdotes or sudden reminiscences to add depth and colour to her mother's life. Alison Highcroft, née Gardner, had been born in 1925 in Torbay. At 18 she enlisted in the WAAF, being stationed somewhere in the East Midlands, before seeing out the war near Great Yarmouth. Somewhere in that period she'd had a brief, passionate affair with a young RAF officer, but he'd been re-stationed and they had lost touch. After the war Alison returned to Torbay to live with her parents, where everything gets very sketchy. At some point Alison's parents died. Anna had never seen any pictures of this period or her grandparents, but she'd never thought to ask or look.

The next event that Anna knew about was that around 1955 her mother had met up with her war-time love. His first marriage had failed, and he was back visiting his mother in Paignton. They met at the sailing club, discovered a shared love of the sea, and married two years later after his divorce finally came through. Anna, their only child, was born in January 1959. But Anna was never to know him. In July that year his sailing dinghy had been caught in a squall off Portland Bill and capsized. Her father had drowned, and his body was never recovered. There was no grave to visit.

Her mother never remarried, and suffered from lengthy bouts of depression throughout Anna's childhood. There was little community network, and no family support. Looking back Anna felt she bootstrapped herself into the world. She left home at 18 and headed for London. She had no idea what she was going to do - maybe join a punk band, or get into journalism, or join protest marches. It was a fluid time.

As she approached the entrance of the Imperial War Museum she was struck by her own unease. She was at once impressed and repelled at the sight of the pair 15 inch naval guns pointing above her head. Symbols of aggression, yet seemingly standing in defence of the traditions of an island nation. Being British was for her a struggle between the legacy of empire, brutal and arrogant, and a sense of fairness and openness. She always hoped the latter was the real country she had grown up in. She had been surprised while living in Germany to learn her country was seen as a saviour and defender of democratic principles. Enoch Powell, the National Front, and other racist groups had come and gone, successfully put back in their boxes. She was proud to have been on the Anti-Nazi League marches in the late 70s, the landmark concert at Victoria Park with Billy Bragg, The Clash. But she worried that the fascist undercurrent would never disappear, and would find a way to resurface. This museum seemed to embody both extremes, and lurking under the surface was a militarist tendency, one that might just start a fire. She'd seen it with the Falklands War, albeit from a distance, and while she was distracted by personal events. But the feeling of jingoistic jubilation was palpable through the TV news footage. She didn't share in it, and cringed at what her German friends might think. In fact, they took it for granted that the British would send an army and retake the islands. She recalled a conversation with Aaron the night the British victory was announced.

'See,' he said, 'they got them back. I told you they would.'

'They wouldn't have needed to if they'd read the signs. It looks like they let it happen. It's taken Thatcher from being despised to being a war leader. And now she's going to get voted in again.'

'You're full of conspiracy shit, Anna. No-one plans this stuff. And your Mrs Thatcher had no option. And no guarantee of winning'

'Not my Mrs Thatcher. She's used the military to keep power. I don't trust her - or any of her crew.'

Entering the museum armed with her ambivalence she went to speak to the receptionist.

'I've an appointment with the Records Office. I hope they're actually here.' She was collected by a woman who introduced herself as herself Hillary, that she guessed was around her own age, and not what she imagined. What had she expected? That they all ran around in pretend uniforms and saluted each other? This woman seemed more suited to the British Museum, or an art gallery. Maybe a curator is just a curator. It doesn't really matter to them what they curate.

They sat down in a small meeting room with some brown loose leaf folders and card readers laid out on the table.

'From what you told me I've dug out the recruitment records of all the Highcrofts I could find. You said you thought it was probably the RAF, but I've pulled other services too. The card files help you locate the history of the regiment or unit if the individual records link a person to one. That way you can start to trace their movements through the war. The best place to start are the enrolment lists, where you can see which individuals signed up where and when. Then you have to follow each person through to see if they fit the profile you have.'

'I don't really have a profile. Just East Midlands, and generally close contact with the WAAF'

'Doesn't rule out the Army, you know. There were regiments posted all over for training and special services. There was quite a lot of mixing. But I'd say the Navy is unlikely. I'll leave you to get started. If you need anything I'm over the hall in that office over there.'

Oh God, thought Anna, what have I started? She looked at the first list of names. Oh well, let's start eliminating the no-hopers.

☐

Chapter 4

Market Deeping, June 1943

ACWs Eleanor Durie and Shelagh Bell sat outside the Wagon and Horses on a warm Thursday evening in June trying to make sense of the day's events. Mostly little happened in the villages of Langtoft and Market Deeping, and while today hadn't seemed momentous, there was a strange sense that things were beginning to change. There had been a lull in Luftwaffe activity over the East Midlands in recent months, and while air traffic out of RAF Wittering had continued unabated, casualty rates had been falling among the air crews. But the last week had seen a spike in coastal raids, and the aircraftwomen had been working extra hours as the interception teams monitored the activity, and guided in the defence fighter squadrons towards their targets. But it wasn't this increase in workload that troubled them. Rumours were rife that the command structures were being broken up, and there was talk of a new air force being set up. What concerned these young women was the possibility of being reposted.

It wasn't as if they had a particular attraction to this corner of Lincolnshire with its featureless flat fields, straight roads and wind-blown remote settlements, but they had been here a while and made some good friendships. And besides, they really did feel they were contributing to the active defence of the realm, providing key communications to the fighter defence squadrons. Ground-controlled interception did not sound exciting, but they had met a good number of air crews, and heard first-hand stories from pilots about how GCI had saved their lives, or managed to drop them right on top of the enemy giving them the upper hand. Of course, they mostly got the impression that these young men that regaled them with their heroics were playing to the gallery, and flattering the women for attention and admiration, rather than trying to boost morale. But it was good to hear nevertheless.

Eleanor in particular didn't like the idea of moving again. When she first arrived in the area she had been billeted on the Measures' farm south of Market Deeping. Frank and Hilda Measure had taken to the young south London woman due to her warm nature and intensity. While she seemed to harbour a slight air of credulousness, there was a mysteriousness. She could quote lines of obscure texts about spirituality or from forgotten poets. Her father traded in antique books, which gave her access to some rare and unusual literature, some snippets of which she liked to share with people, on the off-chance they could help her determine the hidden meanings she felt were just out of reach. This, despite a natural shyness, drew attention to her. Wherever she had travelled during this war she had established bonds that survived the inevitable separation that went with an itinerant WAAF life. First there was the barracks in Morecambe where the new trainees were crammed together, and then Mrs Young in Southwell. And with the Measures, and their farmer friends the Marrs, she developed a deep relationship.

In addition there was another connection she didn't want to lose, and it was to this that their conversation turned, having exhausted the speculation on the meaning of 'The Second Tactical Air Force'.

'So does our commanding officer know any more about these rumours?' Shelagh asked.

'Howard? I don't know I haven't spoken to him properly for a couple of weeks. He's been away on leave.'

"Oh, I'm surprised you're not in his office every day, he's taken a real shine to you.'

'It's not like that, and you know it. He's happily married. He's become a bit of a family friend. I'm not quite sure why Daddy gets on so well with him. He's a real firebrand, Labour Party member and all that. Sometimes I think he's even a bit of a pacifist. I'm not sure if he'd tell me any military secrets, though.'

'I'm not sure the rumours are secrets. Everyone knows we're going to invade Europe now the Yanks are here.'

'Well I might ask him at the weekend what he knows, he said he'd take me out for my birthday.'

'Is that wise? He shouldn't be doing that you know. There'll be talk.'

'It's fine, Shelagh darling. I've met his wife. We all went out when she came down from Nottingham on leave last time. She knows she can trust her man.'

'Talking about leave, I had a note from Edmee. Apparently there's a midsummer bash over at Staythorpe, do you fancy going? A late birthday party for you.'

'Sounds fun, I'd love to see Edmee. Perhaps we could pop over to see Mrs Young in Southwell. She might even put us up.'

The pair had trained together in Morecambe, Eleanor having enlisted just before her 20th birthday on the announcement of conscription for women. In July 1942, Eleanor, Shelagh and another new recruit, Edmee Herbert, were transferred together to the new East Midlands radar station at Staythorpe, five miles east of Southwell. Their training had seemed so cursory, and they hardly felt ready to be properly stationed when they left on the slow train journey south. When the trio disembarked at Rolleston station they were surprised at the makeshift nature of the new base, set up in the middle of a racecourse. They would soon learn that after dark they needed to plot their route carefully back to the village - it was all too easy to bump into the tote on the way across the field. They were grateful to be billeted in nearby homes through the cold winter, the quarters of the training centre had been basic in the extreme. Then in March 1943, Eleanor and Shelagh were re-stationed to Lincolnshire.

Langtoft was dubbed the 'Happidrome' by those that worked there. Its dour and lonely aspect on the edge of an expanse of fields belied the buzz of activity within. Here the positions of all Lincolnshire coastal air movements were monitored, with direct fighter communications for interception of enemy aircraft. The station was under the command of RAF Wittering some twelve miles south, and the commanding officer Flt Lt Howard Jervis was in charge of the small radar station. Howard was fifteen years older than Eleanor and lived in the same part of south London as her, where he had been active in the local Labour Party before the war. It was his love of poetry that forged a bond between him and the young woman. She had told him that her father dealt in antique books, and he had asked her if her father might have a copy of a Coleridge anthology he was keen to get hold of. That had started a more regular correspondence, with Eleanor as the intermediary, between the two men.

'Howard, where did that beard come from? You look like Lenin!'. They met at the Goat in Market Deeping.

'Aha! Someone gets it!' said Howard, greeting her as she entered the bar.

'I think you joined the wrong political party, you're going to get yourself into trouble.'

'You know me, if it doesn't shake the tree it's not worth doing. Belated happy 21st birthday. I'll run you back to the Measures' later.'

Over a shared black pudding hot pot they caught up on news and the rumours that were circulating. Howard was able to confirm that command structures were changing. The Second Tactical Air Force had been established at the beginning of June, but the details were still emerging. 'It's a new defence force, with a mix of bomber and fighter squadrons and, it seems, the GCIs that go with them. Seemingly a need for rapid relocation and agility'.

'Is that what Staythorpe was all about - mobile radar?'

'I'd say you're right there. And there's new kit being deployed in those bases too.'

'I'm going up there in a couple of weeks, I'd love to learn if sleepy old Staythorpe could be the vanguard of the resistance.'

Their conversation soon turned more introspective. 'So that piece you sent me by that fellow Benson, what was all that?'

'I wanted your opinion. He seems like a wise old owl, looking for the recipe for happiness.'

'I hope you're not looking to find happiness. It's an illusion you know.'

'Aren't we all looking for happiness - and peace?'

'Peace, my dear, is also an illusion. When this war is over I doubt it will be the end of conflict. Europe's been at war for ever. So while nations are all still trying to get the upper hand there is little room for personal peace. It's our moral duty to keep up the struggle for a fairer world.'

'You're such an idealist, Howard. Why can't we just find our corner of the world and make it our own?'

'I think that makes you the idealist, my dear. There can't be real peace until Europe agrees to work together for the common good. I don't see that anytime soon, do you?'

'No, Howard darling. I think you're missing the point. All we have is our own little corner. It's all we can be sure of.'

Back at the Measures' that night she wrote to her father. He wrote to her every week, and she felt bad that she was sporadic in her replies. But nothing much happened from one week to the next. Operating radar had become routine, the war news, such as it was, was known to everyone, and there wasn't time for any developments in her private life. Still, she knew that despite his stiff manner and reserve he was a man in need of family bonds. He had lost his wife to tuberculosis when Eleanor was nine years old, and had to bring up two children but lacked the practical skills and knowledge. He missed his wife every day, and Eleanor understood his pain - she had been devoted to her mother, and together they bore the loss with a quiet and unspoken depth. Her younger brother seemed less affected, but he was a gentle soul to whom she felt a strong protectiveness. She would write to him later too. He had also joined the air force, and was currently undergoing cadet training in Scotland. At least she felt he was safely out of the way for now. They had both endured the Blitz in south London, sheltering under the kitchen table when the bombs sounded too close - they always sounded too close. There were no underground stations in Upper Norwood to shelter in. Sometimes after the all clear was sounded they would stand outside and watch the glow of the bombing aftermath from east and central London. It reminded her of the time as a child that she watched in dismay from her bedroom window as the great Crystal Palace burned just a mile away. That had seemed fiercer, more frightening even. It had confirmed to her then that, following the death of her mother, there were no certainties. Everything could be lost.

**

Eleanor and Shelagh made the trip to Southwell by a variety of buses and trains on the last Friday in June. They planned to stay a couple of nights with Mrs Young, meet up with Edmee on Saturday afternoon, and all three would travel out to Staythorpe for the midsummer dance, which was being organised by the local young farmers association. It was a good opportunity to catch up with friends and former colleagues.

Edith Young lived in an end-of-terrace house on Kings Street in view of the old Minster. Electricity was slow to reach this town, and all the houses in this street were lit by gas lamps. The march of 20th century progress had passed much of this community by, and with war rationing of food and petrol, Southwell seemed like a town gone into reverse, a far cry from its heyday as an ecumenical powerhouse a century before. Perhaps its saving grace was the presence of military personnel that now flowed through its houses, pubs and tea rooms. Edith had lost her older brother in the last war, and her husband had died a few years ago in a tragic agricultural accident. She was more than happy to share her house with the young women of the WAAF for the company, and for a connection to the world beyond. Wireless radio wasn't available to many around here, and news was slow to arrive and was often incomplete. Eleanor had stayed here for eight months, sharing a room with Shelagh. There was another girl staying here now, but there was still a spare bed and an old settee that would serve them nicely for the weekend.

Eleanor and Shelagh met Edmee in a tea room and learned the news of their old station and former comrades. 'It's all change,' said Edmee, 'new equipment, and a constant stream of new people. It's quite the centre of the world right now.'

They heard about the new radar units, the training on assembly and dismantling the rigs, and Edmee's promotion to ACW1. 'I doubt I'll make corporal, but I do get a bit more responsibility. A couple of the new girls report to me - hang on my every word.'

She told them to expect a lively night, particularly now that a trio of new officers had transformed the social scene since they arrived a month or so ago. One of them seemed to have taken a shine to Edmee. 'Don't all officers take a shine to every ACW they meet?' asked Shelagh. 'Well they're all great fun,' said Edmee, 'you'll enjoy yourselves tonight.'

When they arrived at Rolleston village hall there was an assortment of locals and blow-ins. The young farmers association in the area mostly consisted of not-so-young men and a group of land girls. Scattered around the room were several RAF uniforms. There was a small band in the corner - piano, trumpet and drums - and at the far end of the room a makeshift bar. There looked to be plenty of beer. The three women were soon joined by four ground crew from the base, all carrying additional half pints for the girls. Edmee knew them, but they were clearly newcomers since the other two had been reposted.

'I don't think I recognise anyone here,' said Eleanor almost to herself, as she resigned herself to an evening as a spectating wall flower. She usually pictured herself this way, although it was never how her evenings ended up. The four young men had already had a few, and a couple of them were loudly describing their prowess on the football field that afternoon. 'Would you like to dance?' one of the men asked Eleanor. There was no one else on the dance floor yet. She politely declined, but did accept the cigarette the man offered as a conciliation to him. 'Where's your new fancy man, then?' Shelagh asked Edmee, in a pointed message to the young signalmen that they were only a temporary feature of the night. Shelagh was tall and had a way of leaning her head back, thick blond hair rolling off her shoulders, and blowing smoke over the heads of the men she talked to, at least to those that didn't interest her. It gave her the air of being in charge of the conversation, the director of social operations. 'I don't know, I'll bet they're in the pub - wait, look here they are!'

In through the door walked three Flight Lieutenants, one of them in full flow of telling a story, waving his cigarette to highlight some event or other. The three of them were absorbed in each other's company and laughed loudly at what must have been the punchline. Once the joke had worn off, and they had calibrated their surroundings, the storyteller broke away from the other two and headed for the bar. Eleanor followed him with her eyes as he moved down the centre of the room. He had a purposeful stride, in which she detected a slight lop-sidedness, and he had a palpable focus of intent. The other men headed towards the three girls - the group of tech-crew breaking away and fading back, they knew their gifts of drinks and cigarettes had been in vain.

'Vince!', 'Edmee, darling!' The two greeted each other with a kiss. This wasn't just a shine, this was a thing. 'Well you have been keeping a secret haven't you Edmee dear?' said Shelagh. 'Yes, well. This is Vince Reedbanks, and this here is Jerry Mays. And here are my friends Shelagh and Eleanor that I told you about.' Jerry looked faintly uneasy as Vince broke into a protracted explanation of why they were late, which mostly consisted of the fact that their friend currently at the bar had decided to make a new best friend of the pub landlord, promising him he would give lessons in how to build a wireless. Vince was also keen to point out that the lessons would never happen, and there was a litany of unrequited best-friendships the length and breadth of Nottinghamshire.

At this point their comrade walked up to them carrying three pints of beer, with the dying cigarette stub in his mouth. He negotiated handing the drinks to his pals, and took the cigarette from his mouth. He looked straight at Eleanor. 'Hello,' he said, 'I'm Doug.'

☐

Chapter 5

The Birth of Aaron

London, December 1989

Anna awoke from an intense dream. Her eyes still closed, but now aware that she was fully conscious. The first thing she noticed was her heart racing. Is that normal, she wondered? A couple of lingering images re-emerged to grab her attention. The first was of Aaron holding a gun, pointing into the abstract, and second was her mother, or a mother figure, standing behind her watching the scene. Then she became that observer, seeing Anna and Aaron from her mother's view point. She set about trying to recall the whole dream and piece together the fragments coming thick and fast, too scrambled to form a narrative. It would haunt her all morning. A storm drain, a small child, a daubed swastika.

She would have to get up for work, the early shift today. This would give her some time to get back to the museum later that afternoon. She made herself a cup of tea and stared out of the kitchen window on to a grey Roseberry Avenue as a 38 bus went past, the dream gnawing away at her. Did she regret her life in Berlin? She knew she regretted the reason for going there, but it hadn't been wasted time. She'd seen a world she wouldn't have believed existed, learned another language and got an education. But Aaron had turned her upside down, torn the heart out of her.

They had met in the summer of 1981, his arm draped over Molly's shoulders as they were walking along Cartwright Gardens, heading away from Molly's squat on Burton Street. The briefest of introductions. Hi, Anna, this is Gerhard, he's from Hamburg. Anna's the singer in the band. Good to meet you. They'd all gone to the pub, and somehow by the evening she had ended up with him back at her flat off the Balls Pond Road. Molly didn't seem bothered. They never mentioned it to each other afterwards.

He started coming to their gigs - all minor venues - the Calthorpe Arms, the Pindar of Wakefield, they even had a support at the Hearty Goodfellow in Nottingham (one of Molly's contacts). Anna knew the band was crap, but it was fun, and felt like she was part of the scene. A couple of the acts they supported went on to fame and notoriety. They once supported an early incarnation of the Pogues who they hung out with a bit.

Most of their gigs were like the first one that Gerhard came to at a small youth club on the corner of Judd Street. They had been the first band on as the audience were drifting in from the pub next door. Anna recognised most of them from hanging around the local squats and cheap rent flats, but there were a few she didn't know. It always excited her more to play to strangers. Their set went well enough, with a few people dancing and jumping around. Jane the bass player managed to break a string half way through,and while she was really stressed about it no-one else seemed to notice, and it might have even added an extra charge to their performance. Anna spent most of the time singing in Gerhard's direction, as if it was just for him. He kept his gaze on her all the way through, with a smile and kind eyes. He didn't dance, but nodded his head and tapped his foot. The gig was memorable mostly because of the next band up. She'd seen them once before, and they were also from around King's Cross. As they launched into their second number, something about bricks and football crowds, a large burly guy pushed his way through the front and landed a fierce punch on the singer's cheek. The singer went down immediately, he was wiry and no match for his assailant. But for Anna the impressive thing was that he kept singing, even while the big man carried on kicking him on the floor. The other band members kept playing, and seeing their band mate still performing presumably figured the show must go on.

The aggressor shouted a few things and then stormed away towards the exit, knocking Anna's shoulder as he went by, spilling her drink. Aaron sprang forward to grab the man's arm, but Anna managed to intercept him.

'Don't be messing with him, the guy's a psychopath. He'd batter you to kingdom come. I've seen him do this before,' said Anna.

'He can't go around beating people up like that, and he certainly can't be hitting you.'

'Leave it. Those two have got history. I don't know what it is, but last week they were drinking together. It's personal between them, so you mustn't get involved.'

'I'll kill him if he ever hurts you.'

'He won't.'

Anna learned two things from that episode. Firstly, that she felt equal to this guy, and could teach him the ways of her world. Secondly, that the way he looked at her, and his desire to defend her, were things she craved. She realised she wanted some emotional and physical security in her life. Something beyond the relentless anarchy. In the pub after the gig Jane had asked Anna what she saw in Gerhard, who Jane found aloof and taciturn.

'Its quite animal, really,' said Anna. 'The sex is great. But he cares. He tells me that we've really connected. He's right.'

'I hope so,' said Jane, 'sometimes I think he's a poser, but not like those style freaks on the King's Road. Something else I can't quite figure out.' Anna stayed quiet, but knew what her friend meant.

Gerhard didn't seem that bothered by the music or the style thing. He looked the part - leather jacket, skinny black jeans, black fringe flopping over his eyes - but it never seemed convincing (and Anna was never sure about the blue brothel creepers). It was as if he wanted to merge into the backdrop of the London music scene. Something was uneasy, aloof, distracted. But he was attentive of her, praised her performances, wanted to learn from her how to write lyrics. When she complained she didn't really know how to teach him he said,

'But you're a songwriter, a singer'

'I write a few angry words and shout them out over a couple of thrash chords. That's not songwriting. Anyway, punk's dead. People want more than that right now, some sophistication. More heart, more soul.'

After a few weeks, he moved in with her. She was surprised at how few possessions he had, even more surprised to find the only music he owned was two cassettes of Elvis Presley. 'The man had real style' he had told her. It must have been a German thing, she thought, limited access to decent music - nothing came out of Germany except Kraftwerk and Steppenwolf. This view of German music was to undergo a radical education in the years that followed.

After a couple of months of being together she noticed him becoming withdrawn. He stopped wanting to go out, avoided meeting people, and found excuses for staying in the flat by himself. Some days they never got out of bed. He didn't work, and the small income she had from part time bar work didn't give them any spare money for socialising anyway. They would listen to endless Elvis, which drove her mad. She tried playing other stuff – Burning Spear, Captain Beefheart, The Roches – but he'd complain or switch it off. When asked if he liked anything else he said 'I did have a Meat Loaf tape, but I lost it'. That didn't bode well (at least he'd lost it). Their conversations were abstract, half-hearted philosophy, muddled politics. Some of this worried her. Neither of them had a good enough command of the other's language, and they'd spar and parry lots of ideas, but Anna was never fully sure that there was any coherence in any of it. She also felt his politics might be diametrically opposed to hers as he hinted at some sympathy with views of the political right - particularly on immigration ('but you're an immigrant!') and gun laws. She learned that his father was a hunter and owned a good many guns, so he'd grown up around them.

His relationship with his father, it turned out, had irreparably broken down. Gerhard had his own hunting dog, which was injured when out retrieving a duck. The boy loved that dog, and was distraught when he saw the animal had broken its leg. They had carried it to the barn at the back of the house where, to the boy's horror, his father shot it in the head. 'It was never going to run again' he said. Gerhard had picked up a loaded shotgun and held it up to his father's chest. 'I'll kill you' he had screamed,

'no you won't, you little shit. Learn to be a man for fuck's sake'.

At which point the boy had dropped the gun and walked out of the house, never to go back or make contact with his parents again. At 16 he had to fend for himself. He went to Hamburg because of the opportunities he thought he'd find in the city, and he reckoned his parents would never think of looking for him there.

Anna sometimes wondered what she was doing with this guy. He cramped her style - they were going out with her friends less, and she was starting to feel isolated. She tried to teach him how to play the bass guitar, not that she was any good, because she wanted him to apply himself to something. He had no sense of rhythm, or an appreciation of how songs were constructed, but he insisted he wanted to join a band. He raved about her lyrics, and when she tried to explain how she put them together into a coherent song he seemed to switch off. That bothered her because she thought there were some messages she wanted to get out there. She came to the conclusion that the connection between them was something at a deeper level, more visceral. She had to admit that she was drawn to his enigma, his brooding. He always drew her into his confidences, as if she was the only person in the world he could trust. Their isolation in London provided a perfect bubble, and she liked that they thought of each other as special and unique. And of course he was dead good looking, which did bring out the animal in her, just as she had told Jane.

What he was great at was story telling. Whenever he recounted his past, or even told of an encounter at the local shop, he was able to project a picture, put you right there in the moment. He could describe people with brevity, accuracy and insight. This made her a little nervous, about how he looked into a person and extracted their essence, while he himself gave nothing away. Was he drawing on her inner being, draining her personality? Sometimes she felt she was diminished by him. Other times she felt he put her on top of the world, made her feel invincible. It was those moments of feeling powerful that drew her on.

One morning he said to Anna that he had to go out, and returned looking furtive.

"Where did you go, what were you doing?' she'd asked,

'Nothing.'

But he started taking short trips out by himself, always returning looking more worried, never answered any of her questions. She found a letter poking out of his rucksack.

'Are you getting post? Where did you pick it up?'

'None of your business.'

But then out of the blue he'd asked 'How can you change your name? I want to change my name.'

When asked why he said he didn't want his parents to ever find him.

'But it's over 5 years since you left, why would they look for you now?'

But he persisted in his demand to find someone who could legally change his name. They went to a solicitor. It was all very easy, but Anna couldn't help thinking that you couldn't hide behind a name change, there was a transparent paper trail leading right to your new identity.

'It's just another hurdle for someone to get over to get to me,' he'd said.

When she had asked him what name he wanted he said 'I thought Gerald. Gerald Minster - as in Kirche'.

'You are kidding, you're German and you want to be called Gerry? And Minster as in church? Weird. Anyway, Gerald is too close to Gerhard'

'I suppose Elvis is out of the question?'

She stared at him, mouth open, shaking her head. She didn't ask if he was serious, afraid of the answer. He'd stared back, 'What?' They found a compromise - they both liked Elvis's middle name.

So it was that Gerhard Kirche became Aaron Minster. It was a little awkward explaining to her friends that her boyfriend wanted to be called Aaron from now on, but they told people he was trying to build a stage persona. Even though he showed no sign of getting up on a stage.

But in Anna's dream he was Gerhard, the man she first fell in love with, and the emotion of the dream brought those feelings right back to her. It was a full circle, a whole story now closed off. She hoped she had left it behind. Fuck you Aaron, she thought, just let me go. She cradled her tea cup against her chest abstractly, and then drank back its tepid contents, letting the dream images dissolve back into her subconscious. She would study them later.

***

In November 1981 in a provincial town about 30 km south west of Hamburg a small child went missing. It was only a matter of a few hours, but a big search was undertaken by members of the local community, alongside the police. The boy was found safe and well, sitting in an empty storm drain that ran under the nearby motorway. It was connected to a long culvert that carried overspill from a small reservoir about half a kilometre away, and during times of heavy rain, debris would be washed down the culvert and storm drain towards a lake below. The drain collected a good deal of this detritus, mostly small branches or plastic bottles.

The story of the child would have been unremarkable beyond the local community, but for the fact that he had been found playing with a handgun. A real one. It wasn't loaded and hadn't posed a danger to the boy or anyone else. He said he found it wedged in a bit of crooked branch lying in the drain. He wanted to keep it, but the police had other ideas.

A couple of years earlier there had been a murder a few kilometres away at an all-night garage. A man had been shot dead at around 2 am. There were no eye-witnesses, and the shop attendant had heard cars pull up and a short while later two gunshots, and a car drive away at speed. When he went outside he found the injured man dying on the forecourt. It turned out the victim was a known petty criminal from the suburbs of

Hamburg, but there was no evidence that could link anyone to the murder. The case went cold, but left open. Now, the police wondered, did this gun have any links to that murder case? The story made the local TV news in West Germany for a couple of days.

When he still had his old identity, Gerhard would phone a friend in Hamburg every couple of weeks. It was hearing this piece of news, Anna would later learn, that prompted him into action - the name change, the plans to return to Germany, asking to borrow money. It was the last of these that forced the issue with Anna.

'If you want my money, if you want my help, I'll gladly give it. I'll do whatever I can G...Aaron, but you've got to tell me what this is all about. You're not just hiding from your parents, are you?'

That night was a long one. It took some coaxing, some shouting, some harsh exchanges, until he finally started to open up. When the argument had blown itself out, and they sat facing each other across the kitchen table, an exhausted calm settled over them.

'Anna, believe me I've never lied to you. I just haven't told you everything. It's to protect you as much as me. If I get caught then you could be in trouble too. I need to go back to Germany and fix a few things to make sure the trouble goes away.'

He told her the story of the child and the gun, and the suspected link to the murder years before.

'What's that got to do with you?' she asked

'I was there,' he said, 'I brought the gun. But I didn't fire it.'

'What the fuck?!'

'I know how this sounds. Look, I was with some bad people. I was doing bad things. Some stealing, selling stuff, drugs and stolen goods. A whole load of shit. When I went to Hamburg I had no money, no experience, just my own wits. You learn some self-preservation growing up with a father like mine. I was soon running drugs for a bunch of guys. They promise you money, cars, girls, you know. You never get those things, they just make you do more dangerous things. After a couple of years I had become the gun carrier. Small-time gang of crooks acting like they're real big guys, you know.'

'So what about the shooting?'

'I'm not going to tell you anything about that. Except the guy was getting payback. He was told to meet us there, some pretence or other. I was told to point the gun at him, I thought just to frighten him. Then they told me to shoot him. I wouldn't. So someone took the gun and did it instead. Man, I was scared. I thought I was next. Turns out the guy who fired the gun was just as scared as me. No real tough guy after all. We drove off in a hurry, threw the gun into a lake.'

'The reservoir above the drain?'

'Yeah, it was dark and must have got into the drain somehow. I don't know how unlucky that is, but it's really bad news.'

'How can them having the gun get traced to you. I presume it wasn't a legal gun.'

'Oh these guns do the rounds, and the police only have to trace it to one person in the underground and they can start to follow its movements. It won't take long to make a connection to me.'

'What are you going to do?'

'The only thing I can. If they don't have the gun, they don't have any evidence. I'm going to go and steal the gun.'

'From a police station?'

'Yes of course, that's where it is.'

'You're mad! You'll never get near it. How do you think you're going to do that?'

'I have a plan. It'll work.'

Aaron's last night in London was an intense affair. They stayed awake, making love, arguing, crying, talking softly. They both knew this was goodbye. The song that Anna was most conscious of, every time the Elvis tape got back around to it, was Wooden Heart. 'Muss Ich denn, muss Ich denn, zum stadtele hinaus, stadtele hinaus, und du mein Schatz bleibste hier?' (Do I have to, have to, leave this city, leave this city, and you my dear stay here?) She hated it, but these were the first German words she would learn. There was something hollow in Elvis's delivery. The manufactured schmaltz, and sugar-soaked sentimentality. But it soaked into her.

Anna knew that she loved him. She was sure he loved her too. She couldn't imagine being without him. The raw attraction they felt at the beginning had strengthened into a deeper bond that she had never had with another man. Her mother's attention had dwindled over the years due to her deepening depression, so that Anna felt stranded and bereft of intimacy. The last few months had been the most intense of her life, with a human connection she never knew was available in life. And now that he had revealed his true secret, the real reason he was in London, she felt a deeper connection to him. And only she knew it. She possessed his secret. The fact that he was wanted for a crime, which could make her an accessory, felt like an unimportant detail and one she was willing to take a risk on. Whoever he had been, Aaron was different now. He was the man she loved. He was a little dangerous - on the edge, and it wasn't pretend or posturing. Not strutting on stage, but trying to survive. It was probably towards the end of that long night that she had decided to go to Germany. But she didn't reveal anything until he got on the train to Harwich when she said, 'I'm going to come and find you', at which point she walked away. She didn't want him to see her cry. 'No, you can't,' she heard him call after her, 'it's too dangerous.'

☐

Chapter 6

Langtoft, November 1943

Doug stepped down from the truck that had transported him from Staythorpe to his new base at RAF Langtoft. There was a fresh breeze from the east, with the sun making occasional appearances as the low cloud scudded across the sky. The place felt more remote than Staythorpe, which at least had a railway line connecting it to the civilised world, and its air of racecourse vibrancy - even if it was currently unused and overgrown. Here in Langtoft the only connection to somewhere else, apart from the narrow road, was the large ditch that ran along the field behind him. He stared at the concrete bunker in front of him and sighed. He was getting further from the action, not closer. It was something of a let-down as he had been excited for the whole journey. He would be seeing Eleanor. He would be staying in the same location as her. He would see her every day.

The truck had moved off to unload some equipment it had brought across from RAF Wittering, and Doug stood there trying to picture himself in this windswept landscape. A figure came out of the grey block and was walking toward him. The man was tall with a beard and handlebar moustache. He strode towards him with his arm outstretched.

'Ahh, you must be Douglas Highcroft. Howard Jervis, I'm the CO here.' Doug noticed he was also a flight lieutenant and wondered how that was going to work. His COs had always been a rank above.

'I've heard a lot about you, you're quite the popular fellow around here, and you've only just arrived!'

'Thank you, erm, sir'

'Don't worry with the sir, Douglas, we're all the same here. We get occasional visits up from Wittering from the Wing Commander, but that's only if something's gone wrong, which it rarely does. We run a tight ship, but we're all comrades here with a common cause.'

Eleanor had told him that Howard was something of a socialist, and relaxed in his manner of command.

'Well, I hope I can fit right in and be useful.'

'Sure you will, old man. Have you found your billet yet? No? I'll get someone to run you into Deeping, and then you can drop off your stuff and come back to get familiar with the place.'

Doug knew it was not the proper thing to ask, but he couldn't help himself.

'Is Eleanor on duty today?'

'Yes she is,' Howard paused and looked at him, hands on hips. 'Listen, I've heard about you and Eleanor, she's told me about it all. It's not really the done thing, you know – officers and ACWs teaming up – because we don't want things to get in the way of professionalism. But I've also had exemplary reports about your conduct. So my advice to you is try to keep it under the radar, so to speak. Don't let the Wittering lot know about it. Eleanor is a wonderful young woman, and a very good operator, I'd hate for her to have to be transferred out now. She's such a good team player and knows how to make people feel good about themselves.'

'Well, I'm with you all the way there,' said Doug. 'I promise to behave myself. But the truth is it's ages since I last saw her.'

'You can catch up with her later.'

Damn, he thought, how could I be so stupid? In the three months since he had met Eleanor he had no spare moments he could call his own as she occupied all of them. He had written her a dozen scribbled notes, and only received one letter back. One! But what a letter. Informative, charming, witty, intelligent - her personality sparkled off the page. He felt subordinated to her intelligence and empathy. She could see into people's souls. He was sure she had read him like an open book, and found the story a bit shabby, wanting, insincere. They had seen each other once since that first meeting when Eleanor came to visit her friend Edmee again, and she had spent most of her time with him. They went cycling to the river Trent, and took the little ferry across and rode out to Staunton where they had a pub lunch. The next day they had wandered around Southwell, visiting the Minster and various tea houses. The evening had been spent with Edmee and her friends. No Vince though, as he had been called home to see his sick father. After that weekend Doug found himself drawn into her world. They had tried to arrange another weekend together, but duty rotas, respective trips home to parents had put paid to those plans. So when, at the end of August, Doug had decided to put in for a transfer, he was determined it would be nearer to Eleanor, and it was with great good fortune that Langtoft needed an officer with his experience.

Doug did not see Eleanor that first evening. She was working a late shift, and had to get back to the Measures' for a small dinner party they were holding. Doug spent his first evening at the White Horse in Market Deeping with a couple of officers and other ranks. In fact he liked this town, which had more promise and charm than the lonely bunker next to a long drain in reclaimed fenland. He asked the men about the local nightlife.

'Well it can be a bit quiet, but we generally whip up a storm in the pub in Langtoft once every few weeks. But there is a big dance coming up in a month or so, down the road in Deeping St James. Should be fun, with a big band and everything.'

The next morning Doug went to the Ops room to check his rota. As he entered the room he looked around to see if Eleanor was there. Of course she wasn't, as she was on late shifts this week, but a woman he recognised walked up to him. Her long, thick blond hair and height – she was nearly as tall as he was – were highly distinctive.

'Hello, Doug, welcome to the Happidrome' she said.

'Shelagh, how good to see you. The last time was that bash in Rollaston.'

'Yes, that was quite a night wasn't it. Here, I have something for you.' She held out an envelope. He was slow on the uptake and simply looked at it.

'Well go on and take it. It's from Eleanor.'

'Right, yes, very good.' He took the envelope and started turning it in his hands, not quite sure what to do.

'Aren't you going to read it?'

'I will, later perhaps. I ought to be getting to work here.'

He put it in his breast pocket, but had the strongest urge to take it right back out again. He resisted. Better to wait until he had a private moment, although the base was tiny and crowded, so he wasn't sure when that would be. At this point Howard walked in, so ending any desires he had to nip outside for a quick cigarette and to open the letter.

'Doug, good to see you here. Let's show you around and get you acquainted with a few of the staff and the kit we have here. Should be pretty much what you've used before. I see you've met Shelagh, so let's meet the others. We had quite a night here last night - band of Dorniers coming in on a raiding party. Managed to down two of them and saw the rest off with four Mosquitoes. I think you'll find us a bit busier here than up in Southwell.'

They headed over to the control stations when they walked into a young ACW, her arm lightly brushing Doug's.

'I'm so sorry,' he said, 'I wasn't looking where I was going.'

'Oh, it's quite alright,' said the woman, just a girl really, thought Doug.

'Ah Gardner,' said Howard, 'our newest ACW on the base. Meet our newest flight controller.' Alison Gardner, Doug Highcroft.'

'I'm terribly sorry for being so clumsy,' re-iterated Doug, holding out his hand to shake hers, 'I'm not normally such a klutz.'

She took his hand lightly and blushed, not daring to look him in the face.

'Really, it was my fault for rushing. Sorry sir,' She directed this last remark to Howard.

'It's fine, Gardner, about your duties.'

Doug spent the morning familiarising himself with the quirks and foibles of the base, but fundamentally this was all going to be a breeze. Around mid-morning he finally got a chance for a short break. He went outside and found a quiet corner of the compound. He lit a cigarette and tore open the envelope.

Dearest Doug - I just wanted to say how sorry I was that I couldn't welcome you here in person. I've so been looking forward to you arriving. I'll be starting my shift at 2pm. If you are free can we meet in the canteen for lunch today? Love, Eleanor.

The canteen was a cramped affair that could seat a maximum of fifty people in one sitting. It was in a wooden hut set behind the main operations bunker. There were several rows of tables and benches with a single aisle running down the middle of the room. Each table seating six people. There was a single serving hatch at the far end of the room, which meant he had to walk the length of the aisle to queue for his lunch. It was already quite busy, but as Doug scanned the room he couldn't see Eleanor, and he didn't fancy having to sit and make chit-chat with a stranger. He wanted her to be here. It wasn't how he imagined this - he had hoped for something more intimate.

He was considering going outside for a cigarette to wait for her to arrive. What if her shift's been changed? What if she's been called away? He had no idea why he felt so anxious, normally everything was a breeze for him. Easy come, easy go; life flowed, and he bobbed along wherever it might take him. But not now. All streams of his consciousness led to Eleanor.

As he turned to leave the room in walked the young ACW he had met earlier.

'Hello again. It's Gardner, isn't it?'

'Yes sir, hello.' She was looking at him properly now, a little less bashful, he thought. 'I was just about to have some lunch, perhaps we could eat together - both new and all that. I could tell you what I've learned about the place so far.' He detected a West Country accent.

She talked quickly and a little nervously, but she seemed very sure of what she was proposing. There was an intensity in her blue-grey eyes that projected an earnestness and an outward confidence. Her face was framed by wavy light brown hair curling at the collar.

'Well I would love to, but can we do that another time?' Doug's nervousness had overtaken hers. This had thrown him completely off balance, his sense of place and time shifted imperceptibly, but enough to distract him from his main purpose for being there. He hated refusing a woman's company - anyone's company really - but he only had one thing on his mind.

'I'm meeting someone, a friend I haven't seen in ages. Ahhhh! Here she is.' Doug caught sight of Eleanor walking through the door. His world came back into focus. He vaguely heard Alison Gardner say 'Oh, alright,' and sensed her turn and move away, but he wasn't really looking.

'Darling!' he said in an excited whisper as Eleanor approached.

'Oh, Doug, how good it is to see you. I've been so looking forward to you arriving. And now you're here. I can hardly believe it. But Doug, dear, please try to act a little more casually, we don't want the rumours to start.'

'Sorry, yes I know, but I'm simply overjoyed to see you.'

'Who was that you were talking to just now?'

'Oh, ACW Gardner. Howard introduced us this morning. She's new here apparently.'

'Yes, she must be. I don't think I've met her yet.'

They both glanced down the room and saw the subject of their gaze taking her tray of food, and squeeze into the middle of a table of other ACWs. She was a remote figure now as Doug and Eleanor rediscovered the joy of being in each other's company.

'So where's that lovely little dog of yours?' asked Eleanor.

'Pup? He's parked at my mother's down in Devon. I thought I couldn't drag him over here unless I knew the billet would be happy to have him. You simply must come down and meet my mother, and see Pup at the same time.'

'Yes of course I will,' she was laughing, he loved it when she laughed. 'Now let's get something to eat or I'll pass out on duty this afternoon.'

'So what do people do for fun around these parts?' he asked when they had collected some food and found a corner of a table to sit at.

'Well I have to say it can get quite lively. The local pubs are very welcoming to strangers.'

'That's no surprise - we've all got a bit of money to spend.'

'And in fact there's a dance in a couple of weeks down at Deeping St James. Could be quite a night - there'll be a big American dance band up from Wittering. I'm planning to invite Edmee and a few other girls from Staythorpe to come down.'

'So I had heard. Well we ought to get Jerry and Vince along too. I'll drop them a line. Although Vince and Edmee have been going through a bumpy time lately.'

'Yes I know, she wrote to me about it. But I'm sure they'll get through it. You should definitely invite the boys.'

Chapter 7

Anna and her Mother

London, December 1989

Anna sat in the refectory at the hospital staring at her coffee and thinking about another cigarette. I must give up, she thought. She had been brooding over the dream that accompanied her on her walk to work, and wondered why events of five years ago were haunting her now. She thought she had dealt with all that and put it behind her. She wanted to move on with her life. The atmosphere changed around her.

'Anna! Hello, how are you today?' It was Bert, beaming smile, confident swagger and arms outstretched, he transformed any space he walked into. They exchanged some meaningless banter, the kind that served a deeper purpose. It didn't matter what words were said, what was conveyed was different. When one asked 'how are you?' it meant something more along the lines of 'this is how I want you to treat me today' or 'you look like you had a heavy night last night' was in fact 'don't you dare call me madam engineer today or I'll wrap those Stillsons around your head.' Anna and Bert understood each other's code and respected it. Not so Morris who barged through the refectory door with a sense of inevitability, like he was attached to an invisible cord tied between him and Bert. 'Anna darlin'! You look pissed off today. Cheer up, it might never happen.' 'Oh fuck off, Mo' she said. Jesus, she thought, can the man never think of something interesting to say? Does he ever have an original thought in his head? She scowled at him.

'You have got a bit of a face on you to be fair' said Bert, 'here have a fag.' He sat down as Mo went off to the coffee machine.

'Cheers,' she said, accepting the cigarette, 'I'm just not fully awake today. Still dreaming.' Saying this shifted a gear in her, as she recognised the link between the dream and her last conversation with Bert.

'By the way I took your advice and went to the war museum'

'Oh? What did you find? What were you looking for?'

'I'm trying to trace my father, check out his war record'

'Why's that then? Was he some kind of hero?'

'That's it, I don't know. In fact I know nothing about him. But I met someone recently who told me they knew him - back during the war. What was curious was they asked me if I was sure he was really my father.'

"Aren't you?'

'Not any more, no.'

At this point, Morris came back clutching three paper cups of coffee. 'Shit these are hot - clear a space on the table, won't you?'.

Anna's pager went off.

'Hi Anna. There's someone wants to see you in reception. It's the police.' She felt a wave of panic flow through her.

As she walked into the hospital reception she saw a single uniformed officer, who seemed to be intently studying a 'Smoking Kills' poster. As she crossed the floor towards him she wondered if she might faint. Her legs didn't feel that they belonged to her, and she even thought she was in one of those dreams where walking is both a necessary yet impossible task to perform. Perhaps I never actually woke up this morning, she thought.

'Anna Highcroft?' asked the officer as she approached him.

'Yes, what is it?' She cringed inside. That was the wrong thing to say, it sounds guilt laden already.

'Can we go somewhere a little more private?'

Not down the station? She thought, and forced herself not to show any emotion.

'There's a small meeting room down the hall. We can see if it's free.'

When they entered the room, and she had closed the door the policeman turned to her.

'Miss Highcroft. Could you please confirm that you are the daughter of Alison Highcroft,' he said.

'Yes, I am'

'I'm sorry to say I have some bad news for you. Your mother has died.'

She wasn't sure she heard him. He had said something to her, but she was struggling to decode the words and find their meaning. It took two or three seconds to reassemble them in the order he spoke them, and a couple more to understand what he was telling her. She had been expecting something different. She was sure she was going to hear words like 'Aaron Minster….' or 'the German police have asked for…' or 'what were you doing in Berlin on the night of…'. But none of that, just a routine police call to notify someone that a close relative had died. Mundane, ritual, ordinary. This scene must be happening in a hundred places all over the country right now. Only then it struck her. This was happening to her, and it was her mother who had died, the mother she hadn't properly spoken to in years. The one she was planning to confront about her own past. The one she could no longer be reconciled with. So this is what numb feels like, she thought.

***

On the train out of Paddington station Anna stared out of the window as the sidings slid into rows of tenement blocks, on to suburban gardens and gradually to fields. The city slipped away and she became aware that this was her first trip out of London since she had returned from Berlin. She had imagined doing this trip every day for the last three months, and every day finding another excuse to put it off. The journey seemed interminable, and while she had expected it to be an ideal time for reflection and getting her head straight, she thought of nothing much for the first couple of hours. She watched the scenery move by at different speeds, saw rain clouds gather, weep and depart, noticed how grubby the west country farmyards looked. It was when she got off the train at Exeter and was waiting for the connecting train that the familiar surroundings, long since left behind, stirred old memories. The last time she stood here was around nine years ago when she last visited her mother. It was their last proper encounter, in the time before Aaron. As usual Anna had stepped off the train with no expectation of having anyone to greet her, and made her way home – her old home as she thought of it – taking the route around Sands Road. She wanted to look at the harbour she'd spent so many years gazing at almost every day. She had let herself into the house and called out – 'Hi Mum, I'm home' – in much the same way she had done coming in from school. And with the same silent response. She had gone up to her mother's bedroom to find her asleep in the bed, still in her night gown. 'Mum!' she barked, 'I'm home'. The body under the covers stirred and looked up blearily at first, then brightening,

'Anna, darling, so good to see you. Sorry about this, I was so tired I had to have a nap. Go down and put the kettle on, I'll be with you in a minute.'

So much of our lives seems to be conducted over cups of tea, Anna had thought, and so it was that mother and daughter spent the next while at the kitchen table letting their drinks go cold as they thought of things to say to each other.

'Any special friends to tell me about, dear?' her mother had asked.

'No.'

'You do have friends?'

'Lots.'

'You know what I mean? Men friends.'

'Yeah, lots of men friends.'

Her mother gave her a look she recognised as disapproving.

'I have lots of friends who are men. None of them particularly special. It's London, and it's full of people.'

'I know dear, I used to live there. Young people in London have always been much the same I reckon.'

They often had these dead-end conversations where one of them, mostly the mother, was trying to find out something about the other. The stalemate would be broken when someone touched a nerve.

'So are you judging me by what you got up to then?' asked Anna.

'I'm not judging you at all, I just want to know what you're up to. If you're happy. You could be happy here.'

'Mum, I was never happy here. It's a dump. Nothing happens. My friends were all bitches, and the boys were all idiots.'

'And the men in London aren't then? Anyway, what do you mean about what I got up to? Are you insinuating something?'

Anna read the signs and steered the conversation away.

'No, Mum, not at all. You don't ever tell me about your life, so I've no idea about anything. Why don't we take a walk down to the beach?'

The rest of the afternoon had been less testy as they had strolled down to the front, but by the evening the strains resurfaced. Anna had been out to pick up some fish and chips for the pair of them. Her mother suggested they eat the food on their laps in the front room, and as they were settling down Alison started along a familiar path.

'This is nice, dear, we don't see enough of each other. We should do this more often.'

'You could visit me in London. You never travel anywhere.'

'You know I can't, dear. My condition keeps me here, I get too tired. I really can't go away.'

'The only thing that keeps you here is your own lack of confidence. And you're far too dependent on those pills. That's why you sleep so much. If you tried to get off them you would have a much better life.'

'How can I do that? I'd sink like a stone. And with no-one to help me, what have I got to look forward to. Since you ran away it's all for nothing around here.'

'I didn't run away. I'm here now aren't I? I vist when I can.'

'When you think you have to. It's so rare. What do you do up there in London anyway?'

'I have a job, friends, play in a band. We have gigs. We have fun.'

'Fun! It all seems childish to me. Your generation is so self-absorbed. Look at you – threadbare jeans, your lovely hair dyed black and cut badly, eye liner like someone nudged your elbow...'

'You don't get it do you? Our generation - we know how to express ourselves, show who we really are. You lot all went off fighting wars and came back terribly prim and uptight. And still your generation threatens us all with nuclear destruction. We want something new and different.'

'You have no idea. Men went off to war and some never came back. They gave up everything. Brave men. We all wanted something different too, but the world is a big, bad place...'

'Which is why you're so scared of it?'

'I'm not scared, just worn out. I had to bring you up alone you know. It's hard.'

'Hang on, so it's all my fault. Why didn't you get married again?'

'No it was the circumstances, of course it's not your fault. And I never married again because no-one could ever replace your father.'

'I never actually had a father to replace. Did you ever think of that?'

'Here we go again,' Alison dumping her half-eaten fish and chips on the coffee table, 'I'm going to bed. You always judge me and complain, and then run back to your fun and games in the big smoke. Well go on then, go away again. Leave me alone.' She got up, stomped up the stairs and slammed her bedroom door.

The next morning Anna had left early, before her mother woke up. While they spoke on the phone after that it was stilted and measured. Anna never saw her again, but that was about to change.

Pulling into Paignton station she started to consider the practicalities that lay ahead. She would have to see her mother's dead body, formally identify it. She would have to go to her mother's house, her old home, a place she hadn't set foot inside for the best part of a decade. And she would have to do it alone.

She took a taxi from Paignton station to the hospital mortuary. It had been arranged for her to meet the pathologist who would explain the results of the post mortem, and take her to see the body. When she arrived she was shown into a small room, devoid of anything except two wooden arm chairs with worn and faded cushion covers. The chairs, one green and one a tired orange, were set facing each other at a slight angle which, she supposed, was designed to give some sense of intimacy and comfort to the austere surroundings in which people were delivered the most distressing news of their lives.

'Ah, Miss Highcroft, can I call you Anna?' The pathologist was a woman in her forties, white coat, clip board, the very picture of the role. They exchanged a few pleasantries about Anna's journey down, allowing the anxiety to settle a little.

'Your mother died of a heart attack. She suffered a massive cardiovascular event in the early evening two days ago. She seemed to have enough time and presence of mind to call an ambulance, but it arrived too late.'

'I understand from the police that they had to force the door"

'So I believe. We do not have all the blood test results yet, so we are unable to release the body. But we know from her medical records that she was on a range of medication, particularly antidepressants. We are not sure at this stage, but sustained use of these drugs may be a contributory factor.'

Anna was led along the corridor by an attendant through an ante-chamber, and into a room where her mother's body lay covered by a sheet, with only her face exposed. The attendant asked if she wanted to be left alone. 'No, this won't take long' said Anna.

She gazed at her mother's face. It had no colour whatsoever, and its lack of life made it hard for Anna to find her mother there at all. The features were correct, a good deal older than she remembered, but none of the person was present. The mannerisms, the expressions, the way she held her head, Anna realised, were the things that she understood were her mother. This shell would tell her nothing about the life that was now a complete mystery. Anna felt unmoored and adrift. Why? What was different from yesterday morning when she had awoken from a dream about her mother, had in fact become her mother, in full belief that she was alive? They hadn't spoken in a long time, how would this permanent departure reshape her life, and why would it? There was nothing she could say, and nothing more she could do here. There were no insights to be had in this room. She turned and left.

She decided to walk the mile or so to Cliff Road, where she found the familiar sight of her childhood home, a three-bedroom semi-detached house, a few steps from the sea. As she walked up the short path she saw that the front door was padlocked - the result of the hefty shoulder that broke the lock. She still had her own keys to the house, but had no idea if they were still relevant. The police had given her the key to the padlock - no doubt there would be a bill for this at some point.

She stepped inside with a long, slow stride, her body reluctant to follow her leg over the threshold. Peering at her surroundings she was mostly aware of the smell of the place. Funny that she never thought that her home had a smell, and yet she instantly recognised the complex aroma that could have consisted of furniture polish, old carpet, potato peelings, and some added mustiness, and a slight sweetness that she found a little cloying. She moved slowly through the downstairs rooms, starting with the dining room, which showed no sign of having been used lately. She lifted a couple of the ornaments, an empty vase, a decorated plate she was once told came from Greece, an old cigarette box that contained assorted contents of Christmas crackers. Inside the dresser was the dinner service and a small, half full bottle of ouzo. She remembered stealing a taste from that bottle when she was a teenager and vowing never to go to Greece on the back of the experience. On the wall was a copy of the Infanta Margarita by

Velasquez, a picture she always considered hideous, but that also cast a haunted spell on this room. Anna used to do her homework in here as a child, but felt constantly stared at by the precocious little girl above her. The room felt long since abandoned, without a trace of a haunting spirit now.

The kitchen was even less welcoming, having signs of recent life. Her mother had obviously eaten her evening meal, and placed the pans, plates and cutlery in the sink to be washed up. Maybe this was the task she was undertaking that was fatally interrupted. It accounted for that additional smell she had noticed. That and the bin, which she took outside immediately.

The front room showed the greatest signs of habitation. She guessed her mother had spent most of her time in this room. Piles of newspapers, recipe cuttings, a stack of books. On the floor by the sofa was a rumpled green blanket. She assumed this must have been the site of her mother's collapse. The telephone had been moved from its usual table by the armchair and sat, at full cable stretch, on the coffee table. She pictured her mother staggering, phone in hand, towards the sofa and dialing 999 as she slid off the sofa to the floor, with enough breath left to give a name and address.

She noticed a small notebook by the armchair and started flicking through it. It contained brief notes and aide-memoires. Don't forget cat food was at the top of one list. Anna panicked - a cat! When did she have a cat? Was she going to discover an expired moggy upstairs? Perhaps that also explained the smell. Other notes were more obscure - I did have a good life didn't I - In my end is my beginning (when did she read T S Eliot, Anna wondered) - He came knocking on my door again, I know it was him.

She moved upstairs, and was straight away drawn to her old room. It was as she had left it, only tidier. The bric-a-brac had been put or thrown away, but her wardrobe still had her old teenage clothes - the ones she wore before punk began. Her pile of board games on the shelf above. Her old cassette tape player was on the floor of the wardrobe, next to two stacks of tapes. She scanned through them - Now 73! The Guitar Man by Bread, Camel's the Snow Goose. Oh my God, she thought, how shit was my taste in music? Much of these had been given to her by various boys vying for her attention. Well, it worked for a couple of them. But there was no nostalgia here. It didn't draw her back in as she feared it might. She was too separated from that girl now in experience and time.

It was her mother's bedroom where she felt most like an intruder. It was so familiar and yet so alien. The green carpet, and pink floral bedspread were the same as she remembered. And another faint shift in smell. A little more acrid, but definitely a sense of ageing furniture. Her mother kept this room tidy. On the window sill were a couple of photos: one of Anna aged around seven or eight, and one of both Anna and her mother, taken the day Anna had received her O-Level results. It was in their back garden, taken by the neighbour who had leaned over the fence at her mother's request. It brought back how insular their lives had been. No relatives to celebrate occasions with, and her mother had no friends that she could recall. They had looked happy in that picture, which belied the truth of the storm to come. The arguments started soon after that, usually around how late Anna was allowed to stay out, or who she could or couldn't see. Anna had pushed and kicked and screamed every step of her adolescence. And when she discovered boys she wanted free rein to make her own mistakes. She knew what she was doing, and her mother wasn't going to get in her way. Only she did. Over and over.

Anna discovered the truth about her mother's depression when she was around seventeen. She saw the bottle of pills, and asked at the local pharmacy what Lofepramine was for. On learning this she tried to be accommodating, to listen to her mother's point of view. At least she thought she did. But it didn't work. The more ground she gave the more her mother moved in, stole her emotional space, seeming even to breath her air before Anna could get to it. A-Levels complete, Anna decided to head to London and make a life, simply to breathe real oxygen again.

In the corner of the room, under a chair, Anna noticed an old leather binder, with a shoe box sitting on top of it. She slid it out, bringing with it its own micro-climate; it was the source of the fusty smell, flaking, rotting old leather. She put them on the bed and opened the shoe box which was full of photos. Most of the ones on top were colour photos, and mainly of Anna and her mother on various holidays they had taken through the 60s, or down on the nearby beach. But under these were a loose assortment of black and white pictures, many of people in uniform. She lifted out a group photo of men and women standing in what she assumed was a field, and written on the back '9 flight'. She took out a handful and spread them over the bed cover. Another group picture, taken indoors this time, was labelled on the back 'Happidrome, Langtoft'. A third picture caught her eye, a group of three - one man and two women - standing by a poster advertising a local dance. Whist Drive Dance Deeping St James, Friday 19 November. She flipped it over, and all it said was Doug. It was unmistakably her mother's handwriting. She turned the picture back and gaped at it in her hand. Could this be the face of her father? The handsome young man in RAF uniform beamed out at her. He was holding a pint of beer and laughing in a way that she was sure he had cracked the joke - his companions were also laughing, their eyes fixed on him. He was the centre of attention.

So now she had a place and a time. She could locate this man in history. She could follow his progress. She would find out at last who he was.

She turned to the leather binder. It cracked and flaked as she opened it, the dust falling onto the bed cover, staining it brown. She thought how cross her mother would be to see this, but soon realised her error and pushed the thought away. Inside were letters and pieces of writing, mostly in her mother's hand, and more official-looking correspondence. A couple of letters she pulled out consisted of correspondence from girl-friends during the war. Gossip about Canadian flight officers, or complaining how dull the new recruits were. There were other bundles of papers, and she thought she would need to go through all this methodically to see what she could find. She would take this lot back to London. While she didn't have to work for a couple of days, and she knew she was going to have to start sorting out the estate, she realised she couldn't stay here. She decided to go for a walk on the beach to clear her head before getting the train back to London.

☐

Chapter 8

Deeping St James, November 1943

'Well, that was rather intense.' Doug arched his spine as he leaned back in his chair, stretching his arms above his head. For the last hour he had been guiding a group of Beaufighters onto a squadron of bombers as they approached the North Sea. When they thought they had an element of surprise some Luftwaffe fighters had appeared from the south. It looked like they had been drawn in on purpose. The ensuing melee required a squadron of Hurricanes to be scrambled from Wittering to deal with the bombers, while Doug radioed constant updates to his flight crews on the movements of the fighters.

Howard was at the adjacent radar station to pick up the progress of the bombers. He was being aided by Eleanor and another ACW as they monitored and relayed the co-ordinates and movements of the planes.

The outcome was considered a success: two downed German fighter planes, and the bomber squadron repelled and forced to turn back - with just one Beaufighter sustaining some flak damage.

'Well done, everyone,' said Howard, 'first-class work.' It didn't always end this way. The previous week Howard had been covering a dogfight between two groups of fighters. One of his pilots found himself caught below and between two enemy aircraft that found him easy pickings. The aircraft was lost, but the pilot had bailed out, and was later pulled from the sea alive. Howard couldn't help blaming himself for this one, he was certain he'd steered his man out of trouble. But he told himself you couldn't win them all.

In the lull Eleanor and the other ACWs left the room, leaving Howard and Doug to have a quick debrief on the action they had just completed.

'Anyway, Doug, how are you settling in?' asked Howard, 'It's almost a couple of weeks now.'

'Very well. I have to say it's busier here than up at Southwell, although I'd still rather be in the air than down here.'

'So what made you sign up to the RAF?'

'Oh, I wanted to see off the Hun. Make sure the Germans never set foot in old Blighty.'

'The Germans or the Nazis?' asked Howard, 'There's a big difference you know. Good friends of the English over the centuries. Even the Royals are German. The last war might be seen as a family tiff that got out of hand.'

'But they've mobilised the whole nation against us. We have to defend our way of life.'

'You're right there, but don't confuse who your enemy is. They're going to lose, these Nazis. Their Reich is built on secrets and lies, and the majority of the country don't believe it, this supremacy stuff. When it comes to the crunch they'll lose their nerve, they won't have the heart to follow through. But once they lose it won't be over. We'll have to be vigilant for ever. Their foul ideology will rear up from time to time, and not especially in Germany. We'll have to keep slapping it down. But if we beat them now it'll put them back in the box for a while. That's why we're going to need a Labour government when this thing is all over. Make sure we have a country with decent moral standards and sense of fairness.'

'Well steady on, old man,' started Doug, 'I'm not sure having a bunch of socialists in charge is going to keep us safe, you know.'

'If the international working class sees a common cause, there'd be no need for war. Armies would refuse to fight.'

'Sounds a bit Soviet to me.' At which point Eleanor walked back into the room.

"Are you subverting my man, Howard?' she said

'Not in the least. Just sharing an opinion.'

'You do that much the same way a politician does. It always sounds like more of a lecture.'

'You'd probably make a good politician, you do rather tell it as you see it' offered Doug.

'Maybe. I was considering it before the war started. I joined the Labour party, and ran for the council. I wasn't successful, but I might try again one day.'

'Are you coming to the hop tomorrow, Howard?' asked Eleanor.

'Sadly no, someone has to keep things going here - I'm on duty.'

***

A noisy crowd gathered in the public bar of the Waterton Arms. Vince, Edmee and Jerry had got there early and had found a small table in the corner. They had been joined by Shelagh, who was holding forth about the bravery of the Canadian pilots she'd met. Eleanor and Doug jostled their way through the crowd, trying not to spill their drinks.

'I say, could get quite rowdy tonight. Hello, everyone, glad you could make it down to our humble parish,' said Doug.

'Hello you two. You both look very happy. I hope you are keeping your minds on your work,' said Edmee.

'Don't you worry about that,' said Eleanor, 'we're nothing if not discreet and professional.' Vince gave up his chair, at which point the three women fell into an excited and fast-paced exchange of news.

So how are you Doug old man?' asked Vince, 'I hope all's well here.'

'Yes, it's a good posting, good CO, and a friendly crowd. Everyone looks out for everyone else.' There could be no mistaking Doug's cool demeanour towards his erstwhile colleague, with his vaguely askance pose and restricted eye contact. Doug was wondering if he really should have asked Vince to come along, but he knew Edmee or Jerry would have brought him anyway. Jerry was quick on the uptake and steered the conversation to the latest radar equipment they'd had installed up at Staythorpe. The group settled into some kind of equilibrium, before it was time to head out to the dance.

As they were leaving the pub Eleanor leaned into Doug, 'Tell me what is between you and Vince? I thought you were friends.'

'We are. It's just he has a habit of trying to get on my nerves.'

'But he didn't do anything. Is it something he said before?'

'Don't worry about it. It's me being a bit cranky. Vince's a good man.' He didn't sound convincing though. She changed the subject.

'Did you see that new girl Gardner at the bar just now?'

'No I can't say I did. It was a bit crowded.'

'Well I did, and I could tell she kept looking at you.'

'Darling, I hope you're not jealous. I've hardly spoken to her since that first day I arrived.'

'I think she's a bit strange, if you ask me. She seems friendly enough, but seems a little aloof, withdrawn even, as if she's always looking at you from a distance. But she's a good looking girl, and I don't want you getting any ideas.'

'Darling, you're a better looking girl. Don't even think about it.'

'You do a lot of that, you know.'

'What?'

'Telling me what I shouldn't think.'

When they got to the Old Vicarage School Room the place was filling up fast. Grooby's Big Band was in full flow, as was the beer. The atmosphere in the hall was humid and smoky. Shelagh pulled Jerry onto the dance floor saying, 'We never got to do this the last time.' Doug and Eleanor followed them, but they noticed Vince and Edmee hanging back, at first not talking, but then exchanging short bursts of conversation. They didn't look too comfortable. 'I think things might still be a bit rocky there,' said Doug. 'It might be you didn't make Vince feel welcome,' said Eleanor, 'but you could be right. Edmee's holding something back.'

Come the first break in the music the three couples found each other at the bar, and everything appeared to be more relaxed. Nothing a few pints can't sort out, thought Doug. ''I'm just going out for a smoke. Could do with some fresh air.' As he stepped out he saw Alison Gardner walking up the path.

'Hello,' she said, 'I think you've been avoiding me.'

'Not at all. Been very busy in my first couple of weeks.'

'I want you to promise me a dance later.'

'Erm, yes, of course. That would be nice.' He felt awkward, especially now that Eleanor had pointed out her concern about this woman, but he didn't want to hurt her feelings.

'Good. I'll seek you out then,' and she disappeared inside.

Doug finished his cigarette and returned to the bar where the others were buying another round of drinks. The band started up again and he became aware of a hand grasping his elbow. He turned to see Alison standing by his shoulder.

'Here I am, fancy that dance now?'

This surprised him. He thought he could spend more time with his friends before she collared him, but here she was. Doug looked at Eleanor, with mild alarm in his eyes.

'You'd better not let the lady down, Doug, dear. Off you go.' She was teasing him, but it meant he had no way out if this.

'Yes, come on, let's hit the floor.'

It was an upbeat swing dance, which they had to improvise. In fact they did pretty well together. At the end she hung on to his arm.

'We could do another' she said.

'Perhaps later, that was nice, but I promised the next dance to Eleanor.'

'Don't rush off. I was just keen to learn a bit more about you. Someone told me you were from Torbay. So am I. We might know people in common.'

'Yes. Paignton as it happens. I go there to see my mother when I can.'

'Don't you spend all your furlough with Eleanor then?'

'Look, I don't want to appear rude, but it so happens she is my girl, and I'm the loyal sort. I'm sure we can explore mutual friends in Devon sometime, but I really would like to get back to her now.'

'Oh just one more dance.' She was persistent.

'One more, and that's it for tonight.'

Watching from the doorway to the bar Vince and Eleanor had noticed the conversation on the dance floor.

'Looks like your man's been pinched. Edmee's popped out for a while, so would you like a dance?'

Eleanor was feeling irritated by the new ACW, and couldn't understand why Doug didn't just tell her to go away.

'Yes, Vince dear, let's do that'

They walked out onto the floor. It was a slower dance, and he pulled her to him, holding her quite tightly, she thought. As the dance progressed she sensed him becoming more intense in his actions, holding her tighter, and inappropriately low down on her waist. He leaned in to her and tried whispering in her ear. She pulled back, but he tried again. She put both of her hands on his chest and pushed him away. 'Vince, I don't know what you are doing, but it doesn't feel quite right. I think we should go back to the bar. Look there's Edmee.'

Edmee had watched all of this, and turned back to the bar. By the time Eleanor and Vince arrived she had a fixed look on her face, and her eyes were sparkling a little with moisture.

'Vince, I think it's time to leave. You I mean. I'd like to stay here with my friends, but I think you've gone too far this time. Is it me, or is it Doug you want to annoy?'

'Edmee darling, it's nothing of the sort. I don't know what you thought you saw, but I promise you there's nothing you should be angry about.'

'Should I ask Eleanor about that?' She looked at her friend.' Well?'

Eleanor felt embarrassed and didn't know how to respond.

'It's alright dear, I'm not cross with you. I think Vince here has been getting rather tired of me lately, and now it's beginning to show.'

'I don't think he meant anything,' said Eleanor, 'I probably misunderstood what he was trying to do, or say, or something.'

'Eleanor darling, you never misunderstand anything that anyone does. You are the most perceptive person I know. And if you felt uncomfortable with Vince, then I am sure he was doing something that made you feel that way. Don't reproach yourself.'

'I'm going to the pub,' said Vince, 'I'll see you later.'

They watched him stomp out into the darkness.

Over the next couple of hours Eleanor managed to find a number of dancing partners for Edmee. People kept mistaking them for sisters, and most of the time they didn't deny it. The evening turned out to be a lot of fun. With the main tension, the Doug-Vince-Edmee axis, now dissipated, they all found the space to enjoy themselves.

At the end of the evening Doug, Eleanor and Edmee were standing near the entrance to the hall, waiting for Jerry to join them. They had their backs to a poster that had been used to advertise this event. Doug was telling a joke, when Alison Gardner approached them. She had a camera in her hand.

'I say,' she said, 'would you mind awfully if I took a picture of you all?' she said.

'Not at all, said Doug, but let me finish the joke, I'm just getting to the punch line.'

Which he then delivered, sending Edmee into shrieks of laughter. Doug was also amused at his own joke, laughing towards the camera. Eleanor smiled and enjoyed the happy look on his face. Then the flash went off, and Alison said, 'that should be a nice picture,' and walked off.

☐

Chapter 9

Anna in Hamburg
London, December 1989/Hamburg, March 1982

You don't know what you don't know. And you never
know you need to know something until your ignorance
confronts you. Burying a parent is one of these
confrontations. Death had been distant for Anna,
something that went on everywhere but was taken care
of by someone else. It was quickly made clear to her
that she was now that someone else. The hospital asked
who the undertakers would be. Who do I contact? How
do I decide who to use? How do I pay for this? How do I
know if I'm being ripped off? Suddenly she found herself
thrust into sorting out the affairs of a person she had
given very little attention to, someone who could no
longer show gratitude or give praise for her efforts. It
dawned on her that no-one ever would. This was
something that she just had to do, and it came as a
shock after all these years of focusing on herself.

The undertakers, she realised, knew their job, which
was to help the living deal with the dead. All the practical
matters were their domain, and they helped her with the
decision making. Cremation, plaque at the local
cemetery, obtain the death certificate. Was there a will?
Who was the executor? At least she knew these last two.
Before leaving her mother's house she had had the
presence of mind to look in the old filing cabinet under
the stairs. She had found a copy of the will, some bank
statements and savings records. She was the executrix,
although she had no idea what she had to do. 'Get a
solicitor', someone had said, 'they'll sort it out for you'.

It would be some days before the hospital could
release the body, perhaps longer. The case had been

referred to the coroner to establish the cause of death, and now she was in abeyance. Why does no-one teach you this stuff? She repeated this thought several times a day in that first week. Always another task that needed attention. It was like she had joined society, and all these details that had to be understood and dealt with were a constant invasion on her ability to think. Life's so bloody complicated, she thought, even after all she had been through. She almost wished that she was back in Berlin (although, of course, if she was she would probably be heading back to England on the news of her mother's death. Who would have told her, though?).

Leaving Berlin had felt like a point of failure, but she knew she had to do it. Her life in that city had been a rollercoaster. She had been miserable, frightened, ecstatic, all in varying extremes, but most of all she had become self-aware. She had gained a confidence that she could take control of her life, even if she couldn't keep hold of the thing she thought she craved most - love. The realisation that the man she had followed was not what she thought he was hadn't stopped her resolve to win him back. A man might present himself with layers of mystery, but behind them was a real, unconstructed person, one whose raw persona was sensitive, honest and true. This was the belief she arrived at after the initial shock and disappointment of those first few months in Germany. Her initial arrival in Hamburg had been filled with a kind of inner terror, but she was driven by a compulsion that she could not fully explain, even to herself.

The envelope Anna had found poking out of Aaron's rucksack that time had a return address on the back. She had noted it down, unsure why she had felt the need. When she alighted the train in Hamburg this was all she had to lead her to Aaron. He said he would write to her as soon as he found a place to stay and send his address. But two months went by and she had heard nothing. This had intensified her resolve to find him. She didn't believe he was trying to abandon her, it was obvious to her that he was too busy planning his mad stunt. Or maybe the police had already picked him up. Either way he was going to need help. She never considered the naivety of this conviction, or what practical assistance she might give breaking into a police station, or helping him get out of one.

She bought a street map of the city and sat at a cafe outside the train station to locate the address. It was on the west side of the city, a bus ride away. She also checked out city centre hostels in case she couldn't track him down. Apart from a school trip to the Normandy beaches, this was her first trip abroad, and she was surprised at how it felt alien and familiar at the same time. People went about their business the same way as people in London. Apart from the fact that everyone around her had secret knowledge that she didn't, she did not feel out of place. Because she was travelling light she felt able to blend in and be comfortably inconspicuous.

The street she was looking for was arranged with rows of smart tenement blocks, rendered and painted white. A far cry from the weary old Victorian blocks of King's Cross, whose recently painted stairwells gave the lie to the state of the flats (squats mainly) they led up to. She wondered if it would be the same here - who lived in these buildings? What did they do? How did they think? She climbed the stairs to the third floor, found the apartment, and knocked on the door. There was a loud yapping from the other side of the door, followed by some muffled shouts and the sound of the animal being led away and shut in somewhere, its barking still muffled. Anna's heart was pounding with expectation and apprehension.

A young woman, probably her own age, perhaps a little older, opened the door.

'Ja?'

'Erm, guttentag,' stumbled Anna, she knew this wasn't going to convince anyone, 'do you speak English?'

'Hmm. A little,' the woman replied giving a wavy, 'so-so' movement with her hand.

'I'm looking for Aaron. Gerhart. Well Aaron. Is he here?'

'Oh Gerhart. Ja, Aaron jetzt. Nein, no he is not here. Er, he is not living here. Are you Anna?'

'Yes, yes I am. Do you know where I can find him.'

'I didn't see him, but he called me to say he was back and working in a bar. In the centre. I heard about you already – he wrote to me sometimes. Does he know you are here?'

'No. It's a surprise.'

'Hmm, yes I think so.'

Anna mumbled some thanks and turned to leave, but the young woman reached out and lightly caught her wrist.

'Wait,' she said, 'you look tired, would you like to come in. I have coffee. My name is Anja by the way.'

Anna was torn. She was anxious to find her man, but she knew she could do with some help, some touch points in this unfamiliar city. And the two women almost shared the same name, although it had taken a moment for this to sink in. She found herself wondering at how language and accent can add a new flavour and character to near identical words. As she stepped into the narrow hallway and shut the front door behind her, Anja had opened a door up ahead, which led to a small explosion of fur and teeth flying towards her, the previously muted barking now firing up with new vigour. She flinched at the mottled Jack Russell terrier charging at her

'Wolf! Hier! Sitz!' called Anja. 'This is Wolf. He's harmless, but likes to think he's protecting me. Go ahead and say hello, he might try to lick you to death.' Half an hour later Anna found herself on a small settee with this wiry haired, mottled little dog slumped across her lap like they'd always been friends. The first thing Anna had noticed in the small living room was the numerous piles of books – on the floor, on the table by the window, on the small coffee table in front of her.

'You read a lot.'

'Oh yes,' said Anja, 'I'm studying for a Masters in Russian literature. Do you read?'

'No, not really. Maybe some poetry, Leonard Cohen, Dylan Thomas, stuff like that. I like the way words sound. I write some lyrics, but nothing profound.'

'You should try some novels. Dostoyevsky is great. The whole human condition between two covers. Maybe if you stay in Hamburg a while I could lend you something.'

Anna inwardly recoiled, instinctively feeling she was here to help Aaron and leave with him as soon as possible. But she smiled, 'Yes maybe' she said.

In the hour she spent with Anja and Wolf Anna had learned a little more about the mysterious man in her life.

'He's quite mixed up you know,' Anja told her. 'He flits around, and never quite settles to anything. We were together for a while, but it didn't last. We're still friends though. I sometimes think he sees me as the only person he trusts. He hangs out with some unsavoury people sometimes. Perhaps you need to know this.'

'Well I know he is in some trouble,' said Anna, 'and I'm here to help him.'

'My advice is don't try too hard to help. Don't get in too deep. He'll let you down one day. He always does.' Anja was sitting on the chair by the table, leaning forward, one arm on the table and the other waving around her cigarette to emphasise her words. 'But look,' she said, 'if I can help you I will. I do like him, and from his letters I know he likes you. So if you need me you know where to find me.'

Anna came away with a better sense of where Aaron had come from, and his life in Germany had become more accessible. And now she had the name of the bar, but no more knowledge about where he was staying, or what situation he was in. She hadn't wanted to ask too many questions. She didn't know who knew what at this stage, but she was grateful for Anja's offer of help if she needed it.

She went back into town and found the bar, only a couple of blocks from the station. She was told Aaron would be working later, to come back at five o'clock. She had about three hours to kill, so went to find herself a hostel to stay in and maybe get a couple of hours' rest. She hadn't slept much on the ferry, and now that the adrenaline rush had subsided she was exhausted.

The meeting with Aaron did not go as she expected.

'Jesus, Anna! What are you doing here? How are you here?' He'd nearly dropped a tray of drinks.

'You're pretty easy to track down for a dangerous fugitive.'

'Sshhh! Don't say stuff like that.' he hissed.

'Why haven't you written? What's going on? I've been worried sick about you.'

'Yes I know. I am sorry. It's been pretty crazy here. You know, finding a safe place to live, getting a job and everything. Making plans. I was going to write you tomorrow.'

Another waiter came over and barked at Aaron. He told Anna that he needed to get on with his work. He didn't want to lose his job. 'I finish at midnight, meet me here then.'

The next encounter was warmer. They embraced, he told her he loved her, that he'd been missing her like mad. How lonely he was.

'At least you have friends here. I met Anja earlier. What is she to you?'

'Are you jealous? She's a friend, the sister of a friend actually. I haven't even seen her since I came back.'

They jousted for a while, trying to knock each other off balance, but she sensed he was hiding something. He didn't answer a single direct question.

'Fucking hell Aaron, you should be a politician! Have you sorted your problem out yet?'

'Look these things take time. I can't walk into a police station and ask them to give me a gun from the evidence room.'

'But you said you had a plan.'

'I do. It just needs some arranging.'

He changed the subject, 'where are you staying.'

'At a hostel up the road here. But I'd rather stay with you.'

'Oh. That might be difficult. Where I am staying they don't trust strangers too well.'

'Fine. I'll fuck off back to England then.'

'No, no don't do that.' He seemed rattled.

The uneasy sparring went on for some days. They met every day, sometimes arguing, sometimes joking sometimes, the best times, just being silent. This continued until Anna started to run out of money. "I'm going to have to move in with you or go home,' she told him. He said he'd sort it. And he'd give her some money - he said it was about time he started to pay her back.

Anna moved in the next day. He had a room in a flat that he shared with three other men. There was no communal space, so she hardly saw these people at first. But she would see them in the kitchen in the morning, or pass them when she came out of the bathroom. They barely acknowledged her presence, but there didn't seem to be any animosity. Then one day Aaron asked if Anna wanted to earn some money.

'It's easy. And not at all dangerous,' he said.

'That sounds dangerous then.'

'No. You just take a package to a house, that's all.'

'What's in the package.'

'You don't ask. Look, OK it's not legal, but you know the kind of people I know. It's easy money.'

'But it's dangerous, and it's working for bad people.'

'They don't need to be your friends.'

'Is Anja one of these people?'

'No, but her brother is. In fact it was his idea to use you - I mean ask you. You are a new face in town, unknown to the police. It'll be good money. You only do this one.'

She had agreed, and while she instantly regretted it, she secretly thrilled at the idea. At least she would be a part of something - embedded in a culture, even if it was a criminal culture.

The job itself was mundane. She carried a package in a plastic shopping bag to a house on the south side of the city. She knocked on the door, someone came and took it from her, and she went away. No swapping buses ten times, or constantly looking for suspicious characters following her. It was good money too - one thousand Deutschemarks. The second time earned her a little less, DM 800. 'It all depends on the value of the package' she was told. 'How do I know what that is?' 'You don't need to. We know. Trust us.' Which, of course, she had no option but to do. She noticed the payments got less every time. 'Times are hard right now' they'd say.

She told Aaron that she wanted to get a proper job, but he snapped at her. 'No don't do that. If you become legitimate then you'll be known. It's best you stay under the radar.'

'So you just want me to be a mule, is that it? Feed your friends. Anyway, you work, how's that different?' They had argued, but she felt too insecure, too out on a limb to be able to push back. She fell in line and kept delivering the packages across the city. One time she was sent to Bremen, which earned her very good money.

That trip had taken her out of town for a couple of days, and she returned to find Anja sitting on her doorstep, with Wolf sniffing at the pavement around her feet, and growling at the occasional cyclist that went past. When he saw Anna the dog started barking and jumping around her heels until she bent down and made a fuss of him.

'Hi, what are you doing here?' asked Anna.

'I just came by to see you. No-one was in though. Here I brought you these.' She handed Anna a couple of books. 'I thought you should do some reading.'

'They're in German.'

'Yes, it'll be good for learning the language. This one is Hermann Hesse, Steppenwolf. It's popular with hippies, but the language is quite easy. This other one is Crime and Punishment. It might take you a bit longer. But do it. Everyone needs to read Dostoyevsky. So where's Aaron?'

'No idea, I just came back myself.'

'I'm glad to catch you on your own,' said Anja, 'I wanted to ask how you are. How the job is going, and things between you and Aaron.'

'We're fine. You know I still can't work him out. What motivates him and why he got into this life.'

'It's his background, I think. You know he left home when he was young.'

'Yes, he told me. He thought his father was a bully.'

'His Dad was old school. He fought in the war you know. He was in Normandy when the Americans and British landed. He saw a lot of bad stuff. Actually I think he was quite dedicated to the idea of the Reich. He was bitter about losing the war apparently. I think that's another reason Aaron left; he needed to break out of that claustrophobic mindset'

'What about you? No-one our age seems to talk about the war here.'

'No. My parents were too young, and part of the generation who grew up trying to fix a broken country. Most people my age figure we have to get on and keep building a better life. No-one wants to go back to the bad old days.'

'Germany seems to be doing fine. And it welcomes in foreigners. At least here in the West.'

'Maybe. Auslanders and gastarbeiters are here in big numbers, but not everyone welcomes them. There are still some old folk who won't forget. And they won't forgive either, although I think it was people over in East Germany got it worse – Dresden and all that.'

'And where is Aaron in all of this? He never wants to talk politics.'

'Honestly? I think he's a little lost. He came from a small community in the countryside. People think differently there. He might have escaped a bullying father, but not everyone escapes their past.'

Anna and Aaron's way of life became routine. They started to have a pretty good lifestyle. They found a flat of their own. Anna went to language classes. They bought a car and went away for weekends. But Anna started to get queasy by this cosy way of life and untroubled calm. It all seemed too easy. One day she said to Aaron 'Hey, just when are you planning to sort out this gun thing? You don't seem to think it's very urgent now.'

'Well the plan was more difficult than I thought. And the police don't seem to be asking questions. Maybe they haven't traced where the gun has been. Who knows? It's all quiet - forget about it.'

This didn't ring true to Anna. It had been the sole focus of his life, his reason for running away from her. It had defined them both. And now she had to forget about it, and she was running drugs, or cash, or whatever. She had been drawn into his underworld, but she didn't know what the risks were, and she wanted the whole thing to stop. Which it did, but not in a way she had any control over.

One morning Anna was having a lie-in. Aaron had been out 'on an errand' he had said. He burst into the bedroom.

'Anna! Get up! Pack quickly. We're leaving. We have to get out of here now. Anna! Move!'

'Why, what's going on? Where are we going?' she blearily sat up in bed.

'We're going to Berlin. I'll tell you on the way, but we have to go right now.'

'Is it the police?'

'No it's worse than that. Come on!'

They threw clothes and essentials into bags. Aaron explained that Anja would come by to sort out the rest of their stuff. Outside she saw Anja sitting in the driver's seat of their car. 'She's driving us,' said Aaron, 'get in.' Anna slid in the back to find an excited Wolf jumping over her. They drove about 30 km to a small town railway station where they were to catch a train to Berlin. She asked why not get the train from Hamburg - 'to cover our tracks' she was told.

As she was getting out of the car Anja turned around from the driver's seat and grabbed her arm. 'Anna,' she said, 'be careful. Don't do anything in Berlin that gets you noticed by the gangs. Stay clean, get a real job, get into the music scene. And don't let Aaron do this stuff either. When you get a place in Berlin let me know and I'll send your stuff on to you. Good luck.'

'Thanks, Anja. I won't forget this. You've been a real friend to me. And bye-bye little Wolf, I'm going to miss you. Come and see us one day, Anja.' She hurried off to join Aaron at the ticket office.

'So here's the story,' Aaron said when they settled on to the train. The story he told in an urgent near-whisper brought to Anna a new wave of incredulity. If any of it was true, then she had been led to this life on a pack of lies. She knew that one story or another was false, and perhaps it would be impossible to believe anything he told her from that point on. When he had finished speaking she said nothing. They sat in silence all the way to Berlin.

This is what he had told her:

Frank Gottschalg was a big name in the Hamburg underworld, and he had just been released from prison on bail. Everyone had expected him to be locked up for years, but his lawyers had found a technicality that made the up-coming trial look shaky. For now he was free and angry, and known to be very brutal with those he was angry with. He was particularly angry, it seems, with Aaron.

'Why?'

'I'm coming to that.'

Aaron had worked for Frank on and off, but Frank's people were not good at paying. Aaron was owed quite a lot of money. So for one job Aaron didn't show up. He was supposed to run a package across town - money he assumed - for a consignment of drugs that Frank was taking control of. It meant the deal failed. (Aaron pleaded ignorance of the nature or details of the deal). It caused shock waves in the gangland networks of Hamburg, and there was chatter in every bar, which meant the police got to hear.

'So he would have been very pissed off with you? Seems a bit dumb to me.'

'Yes I know. I was angry at them for not paying me. I wanted more respect, and it was time they gave me bigger responsibilities. I didn't know it was such a big deal, and looking back I realise it was stupid. But it's actually what changed my mind about the whole way of life – and that's when I decided I wanted to get out. Being a bigger player is much more dangerous. Anyway, it gets worse.'

The police called on Aaron ('don't forget I was Gerhard then'). There was no evidence of any crime being committed, but there was a large amount of drugs somewhere waiting to find an outlet to the street. It would just be a matter of time. So they wondered what they could learn from this junior runner. He was scared enough as it was, keeping clear of Frank's people, and thinking of leaving town. The police put Aaron under a great deal of pressure. They told him, convincingly, that they had enough to put him inside for a good long while. When asked what he knew about the drug lord's activities Aaron had let slip something related to the forecourt killing, something that a smart police officer could easily join up the dots to.

'But that was stupid, you were there.'

'Well, actually no I wasn't. I made that bit up. I knew the people who were, but me, I was asleep in my bed. And Frank was one of them. I think he pulled the trigger, but I didn't ask too much.'

She simply stared at him.

'So that's when I took off for England. I needed to be away from there. Then when I was in London I started to hear messages that Frank had been arrested. And when the kid found that gun it looked like he'd be going down for life. But apparently the police needed my evidence to make a strong case. I was a small part, but important. So I had to go back to Germany.'

'And you thought that telling me that you were implicated in a murder was cooler than being a snitch?'

'Look I couldn't tell you the truth. I was protecting you from bad people.'

'You were happy to make me think I was in trouble with the police. And now I am working for bad people too, being chased by a psychopath. Jesus, who the hell do you think you are?'

'Keep your voice low. We need to be careful.'

That was the point at which she stopped talking.

'Anna,' he said, 'I promise you I'm a different person now. When we get to Berlin I'll get a proper job, with no more shadows and no dodgy people. I know some cool people in the best part of Berlin. I was trying to get Frank out of our lives forever and I messed up. But the police just put me under so much pressure it was impossible to think straight. You are right that I was stupid, but now I'm trying to get us somewhere safe, and where we can build a real life. Please trust me. I love you and would do anything to keep you safe.'

She didn't respond, but his words did make their mark. She wanted so much to believe him and to make a real life with him that she knew she would give him the benefit of the doubt. It didn't all turn out how she hoped, but when Anna looked back now, she realised that the flight to Berlin had been the best move of her life. Even though she never learned how true any of Aaron's story was.

☐

Chapter 10

Market Deeping, Christmas 1943

It had been a grey and oppressive afternoon, but now the clouds were clearing, the stars were appearing, and the temperature was dropping sharply. There would be a frost that night, thought Doug as he walked up the drive to the Measures' front door. Perhaps snow tomorrow, on Christmas Day - how charming that would be. A white Christmas, this year of all years that would be perfect.

He knocked on the door, which was opened by a man in his mid-forties.

'Ahh you must be Doug, come on in. I'm Ben Measures, it's so good to meet you at last. Eleanor talks about you a great deal.'

'Thank you so much for inviting me. It's very good of you to put up with a strange guest at Christmas.'

'Not at all, any friend of Eleanor's is no stranger here, you're very welcome. We have a room made up for you at the top of the house. I'll show you up and then you must come and get a drink. We've some mulled cider on the go.'

After dropping his bag in his room he made his way back down to the living room. The first things he noticed was the roaring fire and the enormous Christmas tree, and then he registered the group of people. There was Eleanor, standing by the fire looking more radiant than he'd ever seen her before. Her eyes sparkled in the fire light. Ben came towards him with a half pint pewter jug that he'd just ladled full of spiced warm cider.

'Here you go. Now let me introduce you to everyone. This is my wife, Hilda, and these are our very good friends Ron and Helen Marr. They have a farm about ten miles the other side of Peterborough. And of course you two need no introductions,' he said indicating to Eleanor.

The introductions and opening small talk over with, the conversation moved on to the latest news of the war. The rumours of an imminent invasion were rife, and it fell to Doug, as the serving officer in the room, to tell them what he knew.

'I don't know any more than the next man, or woman come to that. Eleanor here has probably heard more than me. It's all terribly secret.'

'Yes,' said Eleanor, 'all I know is they've been shaking up the air force and moving a lot of people around. Howard went off for more training the other week, but he never lets on what he hears.'

'It's true they've been setting up new service units,' said Doug. 'In fact radar has now got it's very own active mobile control centres. Apparently we were testing the kit up in Southwell before I came here. It's all ready to be deployed. There would be no point in mobile radar if it wasn't going to be part of an invasion force. Having front-line radar to guide air support of the ground troops will be hugely important.'

'That sounds impressive,' said Ron Marr, 'who's going to operate that?'

'GCI crew like me,' said Doug. He started toying with his drink, and nervously flicking his cigarette into the ashtray. 'As a matter of fact I was planning to apply for one of the units.'

'Oh!' Said Eleanor. She glanced at him before looking quickly away, 'you didn't say anything.'

'Err, no, I've only just thought about it. Sorry, old girl, I was going to tell you when the opportunity arose. There's nothing definite yet.'

There was an awkward silence, broken when Daphne announced that dinner would be ready in ten minutes, so everyone was to be sure to refresh their glasses.

'I say, rib of beef. I haven't seen anything like that for a while,' said Doug.

'Yes, a friend of ours raises Herefords. We managed to get him to put something by for us. One of the few perks of farming in wartime. We have goose for tomorrow.'

'I am being spoiled. The food at the mess is rather grisly, and meagre portions too. It's a wonder we have any strength to fight the enemy.'

'Doug, dear, you are exaggerating,' said Eleanor, 'I think they feed us rather well. When my poor father writes to me he describes his weekly rations. I don't know how anyone survives on civvy street.'

'Perhaps after we take the fight to the Hun things will get a little easier. More supplies from the Yanks getting through,' ventured Ron.

'I doubt it,' said Helen Marr, 'the Americans always seem keener to look after themselves. It's taken them long enough to get into this war.'

'So, Doug,' said Ben, leaning into the table, 'do you think the Americans will help us win this thing?'

'Well they do have a lot of men here now. There's no doubt about the plan to invade Europe. They've got the fire power. I think it's all a matter of logistics. Can we win away from home? But actually I think we will, because we have to.'

'People are all rather tired of the war now. Most of us just want it to be over,' said Daphne.

'Well it won't be quick, but Jerry's pretty worn out too. We've been bombing their industrial heartlands heavily for some time.'

'I want to know what happens after it's all over. What we do when we've beaten them,' said Helen.

'Line up all the Nazi leaders and shoot them, I say,' said Ron.

'You can't do that. There would need to be a trial, surely,' said Eleanor.

'Friends of ours have lost their sons. Unimaginable horrors and tragedies. It's unforgivable that the Germans start this war and all the suffering. They can't go unpunished,' said Daphne.

'No, I agree. They must be punished. But through some rule of law.' said Eleanor

'But there isn't any international law. What courts would you try them in?' said Ben.

'We'll have to invent something,' said Doug, 'it's not beyond the wit of man to deliver proper justice.'

'Well, whatever happens I, for one, will never forgive them,' said Helen.

'Doesn't it depend who or what you need to forgive?' asked Eleanor, 'I mean they can't all be bad people.'

'You young folk. You are rather idealistic. I think you'll find as you get older that the world is a harder place. Forgiveness doesn't come so easily,' said Ron.

'I think we will need to repair this broken world. Whatever it takes.' said Eleanor.

'Well said, darling,' said Doug, 'but we have a way to go before we can do that.'

Later that evening, after the Marrs had left, and their hosts had gone to bed, Doug and Eleanor were together by the fire, each with a small nightcap of whisky.

'Alone at last!' said Doug, 'I can hardly believe it. We're never alone. It drives me crazy.'

'Yes, cheers,' said Eleanor, holding up her glass and clinking it against his. There was a short silence.

'So when were you going to tell me?' she said.

'Tell you what? Oh, that. The transfer. Look, it hasn't been decided. I only just heard about it, from Vince as a matter of fact. They're establishing these units and looking for experienced operators. I think both Jerry and Vince are applying. I bet Howard will too. It's a real chance to do something more positive in this blessed war.'

'It will be dangerous.'

'There are lot of chaps out there putting their lives on the line every day. And I'm sitting here with all the other wingless wonders twiddling my thumbs. It's not right. Ever since I was shot down I have been desperate to get back into the action. And this would be my chance.'

'It's different though. You'll be on the ground, in enemy territory. They'll be shooting at you.'

'Darling, it won't be like that. By the time we're on the ground it will be Allied territory. In fact all the action will be miles away. We'll be somewhere guiding air cover operations from a safe place. I promise you. But at least I will be doing something.'

'How long will you be away, if you go?'

'I don't know, for as long as I'm needed. But when this war is over I'll come back. And then we can spend as much time as we want together. Imagine that. War over, and you and me with all the time and choices in the world.'

'Yes, it would be wonderful. And what would you choose.'

'Darling, I choose you! We could get married!'

Eleanor went quiet and looked at him searchingly. 'Married. Doug, are you proposing?'

'Proposing? Yes, yes I suppose I am. Erm, I should do this properly, shouldn't I? Eleanor, darling, will you marry me?' He slid off the sofa on to one knee, taking her hand in his. 'I'm afraid I don't have a ring, but I'll get one. I wasn't planning this tonight. '

'Do you mean it? I sometimes can't tell when you are joking.'

'I wouldn't joke about this. Of course I mean it. Please say yes.'

'Yes,' she said, with a broad smile, 'of course I will.'

***

January 1944 was not exceptionally cold, but dull and overcast for the main part, with frequent bouts of extended rain. This reduced the air activity in the region, and everything seemed quiet in the backwaters of Langtoft and Market Deeping. Doug was increasingly restless and irritable. It was in the last week of the month that Howard summoned Doug to his office.

'Your transfer has come through. You're being assigned to GCI 15082 at Hibaldstow, part of 21 Base Defence Wing. It's a forward operations unit. Congratulations.'

Forward operations, thought Doug, finally a chance to get back in the fray with mobile radar control to support fighter cover on the front line.

'Thank you, sir. I'll be sorry to leave here, but I feel I've more to offer.'

'Yes, I know. In truth I'd put in for this myself, but it appears they want me to stay here. I had rather hoped it would be me waving farewell. But I do wish you the very best of luck with it.'

'When do I go?'

'First thing next week. You might have a chance for a spot of leave, visit your mother and such, but it's a tight time frame.'

As Doug walked back to the Ops room he was wondering how he was going to break this to Eleanor, and how he was going to fit in a dash to Devon. Life was so bloody complicated, and in wartime you just had no control over things. He resolved to travel the next day to see his mother, which meant he needed to find Eleanor now to explain. He hadn't told her that he'd put in for the transfer because he was convinced he wouldn't get it. He didn't want to worry her unduly. And now it was all far more rushed than he had anticipated.

Eleanor had travelled home to London after Christmas to spend New Year with her father and brother. Once she arrived Max had showed her excitedly where the incendiary device had crashed through the roof and made a mess of their father's study. It hadn't exploded, but there was a large hole to repair, and it had destroyed his desk and pulled over a couple of the bookcases. Then the rain had done the rest, ruining some of his most valued books and manuscripts. There was a temporary patch on the roof, and it had been straightened out and cleaned, but it still smelt damp and musty. They counted their blessings that no-one had been hurt.

She felt guilty at that. She was safer away in the Lincolnshire countryside doing her bit to fight the enemy, but it seemed the ordinary population were the front line in this war. She wished it could be over, despite the fact that she had enjoyed leaving home and making all these new friends. War was a mess of contradictions.

And now she had Doug to worry about. Firstly that she should tell her father about him, and then that he was going to abandon her on some wild adventure. Why did men want to throw themselves into the front line? But someone had to, and she was secretly proud that her man had the courage to do whatever he felt he had to do.

In the end she told her father that she had met a man that she was fond of, but didn't go into any details. Certainly not about their plans to marry. He didn't press very hard to learn more about Doug or their relationship. Just enough to satisfy himself the man wasn't a complete scoundrel. Max, on the other hand, pestered her for more information. He was due to enter the RAF cadets in a couple of months' time, and he was impressed that she knew a pilot. Where was he stationed when he was flying? What planes did he fly? How did he get injured? Could he build a radio from scratch? (Max could). To get him to stop asking more questions she said 'you'll have to come up to Deeping and ask him yourself'. They fixed on a weekend in March when Max would visit her.

When she returned to Langtoft she found the atmosphere depressing and dull. She had been excited to get back to work, and most of all to see Doug. Maybe she could persuade him to stay at the station, and they could start making plans. But she soon saw that Doug was preoccupied, and their shifts meant that they had little time together. The humdrum of station life got in the way of what she saw as their real lives. When Doug finally made the effort to make time for her it was a bigger blow than either of them expected.

'Darling,' he said when she walked into the Waggon and Horses and found him sitting by the window, 'at last we can have some time together.' But it wasn't the quality time that she was hoping for, in a pub at the end of a shift. He might have arranged something a little more romantic. And then things went from bad to worse as he explained. He was going on leave tomorrow to see his mother. Then he would be travelling to Hibaldstow for his new posting. It tumbled out of him in a garbled fashion, and he knew this wasn't how he wanted to tell her.

'So you put in for a transfer and didn't tell me? Again,' she said.

'Umm.'

'And it came through today?'

'Umm, yes.'

'Where's Hibaldstow?'

'It's up the road, well it's north of the county.'

'Lincolnshire's huge, that's a long way away.'

'I'll get to see you as often as I can. It's up the A1.'

'How long will you be there?'

'I don't know. I think we'll be relocated at some point, but I haven't any more info on that yet.'

'And then you'll be off to France.'

'I don't know when, but that is the idea I suppose.'

'Of course that's the idea, Doug. That's the whole point isn't it.'

'Look, darling, it's a war.'

'I know it's a ruddy war, you don't have to tell me. My family was nearly wiped out by a bomb last month. I know we've got to win this thing. And I know someone has to go and fight. I just wish it didn't have to be you, when you could make a perfectly decent contribution right here.'

'Gosh, you're angry. I haven't seen you angry before.'

'Well you have now. But I'm worried too.'

'I promise to be careful. How about that?'

'Were you careful flying that plane?'

'That was bad luck. Lightning never strikes twice.'

***

On the Eastern Esplanade Doug, his mother and Pup braved the elements. The dog not so much braving, but revelling. It was low tide and he was running between the barbed wire and bollards down to the water's edge, usually after some seagull or other, and then back to them, urging them to join him at the edge of the surf. The wind was moderate and carried occasional bursts of rain. It was mid-morning, but there was almost no-one else here by the beach, only a couple of other hardy dog walkers. He wanted to avoid another conversation like the one with Eleanor, so Doug kept moving the conversation from one subject to the next. First some detail about the radar equipment, then anecdotes about the men in his charge, before flitting to questions about his old school friends, at least the ones whose mothers his mother had stayed in contact with. It was, of course, a litany of who joined which service or regiment. There were grim stories of casualties, some worse off than him and a couple of tales of bravery.

'How long will you be away?' his mother asked before he could change the subject again.

'Who knows? How long is James going to be off in Africa? These things are out of my hands.'

'We're not discussing your brother, we're talking about you. And I want to know if your job will be done quickly, or if you'll be needed back in England.'

'Once we're out in France there will need to be air cover all the way, so radar is going to be essential. But we're always based well behind enemy lines. The only danger will be from enemy aircraft, and that's my job to spot them. So you see, mother dear, I'll not be in any real danger.'

'When is this all going to happen?'

'The summer I expect. Longer days, better weather. But I don't think they'll tell us until a few days before. It's got to be a surprise.'

'They must be expecting something, the Germans.'

'They will be, but we don't want them being too prepared now, do we?'

His mother stopped and stared out at the English Channel in front of them. There was no clear horizon, and the sea looked unforgiving. 'I can't bear the thought of you having to sail across that water.'

'Mother, right now I'm further away from you up in Lincolnshire. It's like a foreign land up there.'

'Yes, dear, but a friendly one.'

'It'll be different when I get to Yorkshire.'

☐

Chapter 11

Who's Harry?
London and Paignton, December 1989

On the train back to London from Paignton, Anna had taken out the photo of Doug and stared at it for a long time. Could this really be the face of her father? Could she see anything of herself in his features or expression? She had the sense of someone lively, energetic, and full of mischief. She examined his companions, two women caught in a moment of rapture. One had her head thrown back, mouth open in what would have been a loud laugh. The other, dark wavy hair to her collar, had a broad open smile, but her eyes looked at the man more intently, searchingly. Despite the animation of the picture, this woman had a stillness and calmness, perhaps a little reserve. There was little doubt, thought Anna, that this woman was in love with the man she was looking at. Anna resolved to redouble her efforts to trace him, especially now that she had something tangible.

The solicitor was based in Torquay and would handle probate. This freed up Anna and gave her some thinking space. She asked for time off work so that she could focus on delving into her past. She knew she couldn't move forward without this journey back in time. She returned to the Imperial War Museum, but soon discovered that the records were too patchy, and not filed in a way conducive to tracing an individual, or the movement of personnel between military units. She had at least located a Douglas Highcroft, who joined the RAF Volunteer force in 1941, but there was no way to follow his progress. The museum assistant suggested the Office of Public Records at Kew, where the National Archives included comprehensive military records.

At the Holloway Road library she looked at an atlas of Great Britain, which showed the little hamlet of Deeping St James abutting the town of Market Deeping in Lincolnshire. She realised she knew nothing of the way the RAF was set up, but at least, she figured, there must have been an RAF base near this town. It was at the Records Office that she finally made some progress. A list of RAF bases in Lincolnshire gave her locations at Wittering and Langtoft, with the latter being a mile up the road from Market Deeping itself. Here was a physical place that matched with a black and white picture in another world, separated from her own by a fog of myth and ignorance.

Langtoft, 'the Happidrome' as it was called in one correspondence, was a ground control intercept unit under the command of RAF Wittering. She had to delve around to learn what a GCI was, and what it did. She had no understanding of how radar was used to guide the flight crews. The GCI, part of 10 Flight, was commanded by Flight Lieutenant Howard Jervis. There were duty rosters and lists of personnel, mainly showing the ACWs. Anna scoured these lists, and in one found her mother's name, Alison Gardner, but it was undated. There were operations record books. These included details of new officers joining the station. On 1st October 1943, one Flt/Lt Douglas Highcroft arrived at RAF Langtoft. There they both were! This was where her parents had first met! She knew that she had to visit this place.

There was one other fortuitous piece of information. Inside the Langtoft operations book there were the occasional hand-written notes. Next to the entry for 6th February 1943, when Howard Jervis has assumed command, someone had scribbled the words 'later to be MP'. Clearly this was written in after the war. It gave her the idea that perhaps some of these people were still alive, and maybe she could track this man down and talk to him.

She was beginning to think more about what the 'ghost' had told her in the pub. 'Ask your mother the truth about your father. If she won't tell you find someone who will.' When she had asked how she would do that he had said 'try following his war record.' Now that her mother was dead she had no-one else to ask. Until now.

It did not take her long to find her man. She thought she vaguely recognised the name, perhaps some minister or other. The National Archives again proved to be the right place to look. Records of MPs and ministers were relatively easy to track down. Sure enough, Howard Jervis had been Arts Minister, 1974-76. He was now in the House of Lords, Baron Jervis of Greenwich. Shit, she thought, how do I get to speak to a Lord? 'Try phoning the Houses of Parliament,' one records assistant suggested.

So she did. She was put through to Lord Jervis's office, where she found herself stumbling through some explanation about why she should meet with the peer as soon as possible. Was it on some constitutional matter, or perhaps she was interested in his anti-nuclear weapons works? No, it was a personal matter, and it related to his time in the RAF and his knowledge of her parents. She was asked to leave a contact number and address, and they would see if Lord Jervis could fit in an appointment. They would be in touch. That was lame, she thought, and reckoned she would have to go back to the records office and look for other likely candidates to track down.

***

On a whim she bought a ticket to Market Deeping. The bus from Peterborough station dropped her at the Waggon and Horses pub in Langtoft. It was 11:30 in the morning and the pub was just opening. She went inside and wandered up to the bar, where a woman was busying herself with emptying a dishwasher and stacking glasses. The room was otherwise empty.

'Excuse me, can you tell me where the old RAF radar station is?'

'Oh, there's not much left of that' the woman said, 'it's out on the Six Score Road, by the Drain. But it's a breaker's yard now.'

'Is there any of it left, anything to see?'

'I don't know - I never go out there. I'm told it was the life and soul round here back in the day. Best person to ask would be Maggie. She lived here then, comes in most lunchtimes. She'd probably tell you a story or two.'

'Great, when does she come in? And how long would it take to get out to this place?'

'Oh, probably about one. And it's a good 3 miles out there.'

'That's fine, I'll come back later. Thanks.'

Anna decided to take a walk to the site, and see if she could meet with this Maggie later.

She felt she was getting closer to her real past. She followed the route she'd been given, and was struck by how open, flat and exposed the land was. The lane was narrow, but for nearly half an hour she did not see a single car. She couldn't imagine how this place would have been a hive of activity 45 years earlier. It was desolate and gloomy in the heavily overcast January sky. After almost 50 minutes of walking she came to the breakers yard, surrounded by a thin cover of trees. In all directions there were open fields, ploughed and brown, with distant dark edges of the hedgerows. A solitary house stood surrounded by skips, parts of cars and trucks, mounds of unidentified discarded detritus. Behind this was a concrete building that had a large opening that could accommodate large vehicles. She stood and pondered at the sight before her. It didn't look like much, and hardly the picture of, a "Happidrome".

A man stepped out of the house and started walking across the yard.

'Excuse me,' she called, 'do you work here?'

'This is my place, yes.'

'Is this the old radar station? Could I look around?'

'Yes that's right. Not much to see mind. That old building over there, a couple of concrete plinths. We get a few people coming to take a look, but mostly old veterans. Not normally young folk like you.'

'I'm trying to find someone. It's a long story.'

She did not linger. She wasn't sure what she was looking at, and couldn't visualise the activity that would have gone on back then. It was a shell now, with few secrets to give up.

Back in the pub the woman behind the bar looked pleased to see her.

'Oh, it's you. You're in luck, Maggie's come in. She said she'd love to have a chat. Don't forget we close in half an hour'. Half an hour, thought Anna, when are these places going to catch up with the modern world?

Anna bought herself a pint and ordered a sandwich and went to introduce herself to the woman sitting in the window seat, and wondered if she could ask her some questions about the war.

'Yes, I lived here during the war. Never moved away. This pub was always full of service men and women. Busiest it's ever been. Talk about parties! There was something on every night.'

'Do you remember any individuals, any of their names.'

'It's all a bit hazy now, but there were a few alright.'

'Do you remember a Douglas Highcroft, or Alison Gardner?'

'Ooh, Doug, yes! He wasn't here very long - a few months at most. But he really made an impression. Very popular with the girls, and the men as well. Everybody loved Doug. As for, Alison you say? No I don't think I remember her. There were a lot of ACWs you understand. Came and went to other bases quite quickly.'

'Did Doug ever have any particular girlfriends that you remember?'

'Well, as it happens, he did. Can't remember her name though.'

Anna took out the old photo.

'Is this Doug, in this picture?'

'That's him! And that there's his girlfriend. He was besotted. Wish I could remember her name. Nice girl. Where did you find that?'

All the way home Anna tried to make sense of what she had learned. Her parents had met in this place she'd just been, perhaps in that very pub. But it didn't seem like they'd had a relationship, at least not one that anyone witnessed. This man that was to become her father was in a relationship with a different ACW. Where did this leave her?

100

***

Two days later she received a letter from the coroner. Death from natural causes, probably induced by sustained use of antidepressants and painkillers. They would be releasing the body, and she should contact them immediately with arrangements for removal. So dry, so clinical. At least she was now able to set a date for the cremation. She had no plans for the ashes, and the funeral directors had advised her that she could wait to decide this at a more appropriate time. She didn't think a hole in the ground at the local cemetery would be somehow right, but the alternatives escaped her right now.

The cremation was set for a week later, on the Wednesday before Christmas. There was no-one to contact. She thought she might ask the neighbours, but she couldn't think of anyone who needed to know. This will be a desultory and miserable affair, she thought; the fact that Alison Highcroft had no friends or relations that Anna knew of was intensely sad. Anna's teenage years had not been lonely, but she had made all the running - going out with her friends, being invited on other families' trips out. Her mother's insular depression gave her the incentive to get out, but in the end it was what drove Anna to leave home. She now felt immensely guilty at abandoning her mother to her closed world, one that Anna had never tried to get inside and understand. And now she never could. Maybe this was fuelling her obsession with discovering more about her father.

In the end she called Jane. Would she come to the funeral? Did she think Molly might want to come too? The old gang back together? She didn't think she could face this one alone. Molly had a car, and the three women drove to Paignton together. It felt like a re-bonding session, a bit like the time they drove to Nottingham for a gig almost a decade before. For the first half of the journey Anna spent most of the time apologising for running away, trying to excuse her behaviour as some wanderlust.

'Man lust, more like,' said Molly.

'It was more than that,' said Anna, 'I really did want to help him. And I was in love'

'What did happen in Berlin?' asked Jane.

'I promise I'll tell you later. Let's get this service out of the way first.'

At the crematorium Anna met the funeral director who ran her through the order of events. She spoke to the celebrant, whom she had spoken to over the phone a couple of days earlier. They had agreed to a form of words, and some appropriate music. Anna wanted to play her mother out to Aretha Franklin's Respect or Bowie's Heroes, but thought better of it. (She briefly wondered if the three girls could dance their way out at the end to Bad Reputation by Joan Jett, but that would have been like having a one-sided argument with her mother). It would be for no-one's benefit. So some softly piped organ music would have to do.

The room could seat about a hundred people, and the three women and the celebrant were clustered at the front. The coffin was brought in and set before them. The celebrant read out a prepared speech with what she understood from Anna to be Alison Highcroft's high points. The war, meeting Anna's father, having Anna, loving the beach and the sea, sailing. It all seemed brief. Anna read a short poem she had composed that mainly sounded like an apology for not knowing this woman well enough, for not taking the trouble to find out. For her own selfishness.

It was over so soon, and when Anna stepped forward to touch the coffin and say 'sorry, Mum, goodbye' she turned to look at her friends. This was when she saw the man standing at the back of the room. He must have sneaked in quietly behind the coffin. He smiled, weakly, and turned and left. She was in no doubt, but it was the man she'd met in London a few short weeks before. Momentarily rooted to the spot she muttered underneath her breath in a tone of realisation '...ghost...', and looked at her friends in disbelief. They saw her expression and were aware of movement behind them, but by the time they turned there was no-one to see. The gently closing gap of the door was the only evidence that there had been a presence there at all.

'Who was there?' asked Jane.

'It was the ghost - the man who called himself a ghost.'

She ran to the door, pulling it open and flung herself outside. She looked around but there was no-one. She had no idea if he had slipped around the building, or made it into the small wooded copse opposite. He couldn't have gone down the driveway to the road in that time. She went to either corner of the building. Nothing. When the others joined her they had a brief look around the building, but the man had disappeared. They implored her to come back inside. She stood briefly at the back of the room and stared at the coffin. 'Who was he, Mum?' she said quietly.

***

They went back to Anna's mother's house. Her house now, Molly reminded her. They stopped at a supermarket and picked up some food, and several bottles of wine. 'Can you have a proper wake with three people?' Anna asked, 'especially when two of them don't know the deceased?'

'We'll have a bloody good go at it,' said Molly.

The house had been untouched since her last visit, except for the locksmith she'd called to repair the front door. In the front room Jane noticed a picture on the mantlepiece of a young woman in uniform.

'Is this your mum?' she asked

Anna looked at the picture, taken outdoors on a grassy mound, the young Alison smiling and relaxed. Strange, she thought, that she hadn't noticed it when she came in last time, but perhaps because it had always been there. Something she had grown up with and taken for granted.

'Yes, that's her. Taken during the war, I guess.'

'You know you look a lot like her, especially with your hair longer now.'

It wasn't the plan, Anna thought, but she had to admit they were two of a kind.

'Why did you two fall out?' asked Jane.

'It was Aaron. When I told her that I had a German boyfriend she put the phone down on me. Before she did she yelled at me. How could you be so heartless and stupid? – she said – after all the bloody Germans did to us.'

'What, she still held a grudge?'

'When I did get to speak to her she told me she could never forgive. I told her it wasn't my war, our countries were friends now. She should move on, and that I planned to go with him to Germany. And she said if I went away she'd never speak to me again, and put down the phone – again.'

'Was that the last time you spoke?'

'Pretty much. A couple of frosty calls from Berlin, and we exchanged a couple of letters. And now I can't fix any of it.'

She felt the panic rising, that the stream of grief would wash through her. Molly, who had been silently watching from the corner of the room took three long strides and wrapped her arms around her old friend. They stood like that for several minutes, not speaking, not moving, until Molly felt the tension relax in her friend's body as the wave passed. 'Let's get this place sorted,' she said.

They set to work. Anna straightened out the living room, tidying away the piles of magazines and getting some cleared surfaces. She pulled the curtains shut, wincing at the floriferous design. Jane set about preparing the food, while Molly brought in a pile of tapes from the car and made sure everyone had a glass of wine. She put on a compilation tape she had made some years earlier: The Slits, Iggy, Cocteau Twins, some early Acid House. 'Not sure about the Techno,' called Jane from the kitchen. 'Oh just wait til I get out my Berlin tapes,' shouted Anna as she headed upstairs to sort out the beds, 'then you'll learn what Techno is all about.'

As she was stripping her mother's bed she lifted the mattress and saw a large white envelope underneath. Looking inside she saw two smaller envelopes. She shook them out onto the bed. She picked up one of the envelopes and took out a letter.

My Darling Alison,

Why won't you answer my letters or pick up my calls? You have put the phone down on me at least two occasions. I know we parted on poor terms last time, but I do want to make it up. It's been months now, months! I promise you we will have that life together. This time it will be different. I've made some plans, and I want to share them with you. I know we can start again and be completely, blissfully happy. Darling I love you so much, please send me word that you will see me.

My love forever,
Harry

Harry? Who the FUCK was Harry! Anna was saying this out loud. Then she looked at the date: September 1958. This couldn't be right; her mother would have been five months pregnant with Anna then. It was one thing to discover that her mother had some sort of lover that Anna knew nothing about. But her mother was married and pregnant at the time of these entreaties, so what was going on?

The second envelope had a more official-looking document inside on stiff parchment, dated August 1958. A change of name by Deed Poll, she had seen one of these before and recognised it straight away. Alison Highcroft, name formally changed from Gardner. No, shit! Her mother had changed her name to Highcroft?! Wasn't that automatic when you got married? Why Deed Poll?

Anna held on to these thoughts and questions. She knew they would burn a hole through her, but she didn't want to share this with her friends yet, not until it made some sense. She finished with the beds and went back downstairs. Jane was carrying a tray of food from the kitchen, Molly was opening another bottle of wine and refilling the glasses.

'Right you,' said Molly, banging the tips her fingers on the table to emphasise every word, 'take us to fucking Berlin.'

Chapter 12

Church Fenton, March 1944

My Darling,

We finally arrived, and everything seems to be under control. Jerry is here with me, and we met up with Vince again last night. He's been here since the beginning of the year, but I think you know that.

I miss you like mad, it's been ages since I last saw you. I'm hopeless I know, dashing about all over the country. It's too bad you couldn't turn up last Sunday, there's so much I want to tell you. The last time we had together was probably the best thing that's happened in my very short life. Do write and don't forget that, though I hate to admit it, I do love you very much. Will meet you when I dream again.

All my love
Doug

Doug stared out across the airfield through the window of the GCI crew meeting room. It was buzzing with activity. RAF Church Fenton seemed to be the centre of the flying world, with a number of fighter squadrons being relocated here in recent months. It made a sharp contrast with sleepy old Nottinghamshire and Lincolnshire, and the isolation of a remote radar station. He felt back in the heart of things, but still frustrated not to have been returned to flying duties. 'You have some unique skills, Doug. We're going to miss you here,' Howard had told him, '21 Base Defence Wing will be in good hands with your mobile GCI experience. It's going to be pretty intense though.'

They had known for some time that they were readying for an invasion of Europe, although no-one knew where or when. Now that General Eisenhower was supreme commander of the allied forces there was not only a build-up of armaments, but increased training exercises for open field operations. The amalgamation of squadrons on to the large bases fitted this picture. 21 BDW was to be forward operations in the first wave of the invasion force. Doug had first moved to the training station at Hibaldstow, where he joined his new unit, GCI 15082. His new team comprised an assortment of radar technicians, officers and operators, including a number of Canadians. Jerry Mays had also been transferred to the unit, where their task had been to turn the crew into a rapid deployment unit. They would not only practise system assembly repeatedly, but also work with day and night fighter squadrons in practise intercept manoeuvres.

Now he found himself collected together with their designated fighter squadrons, and five other mobile radar teams. The momentum was clear, all this preparation was heading for a big confrontation with the enemy. It would obviously be a summer offensive to take advantage of the better weather, but it left everyone guessing. The adrenaline levels seemed to have a permanent edge of expectation. The base was alive. The easy camaraderie was giving way to tensions among crews as they understood there was a real chance of seeing active combat, and not just supporting it from deep inside the English countryside.

There was a clatter of boots on the wooden floor behind him as the door was flung open and a group of men filed in and spread out across the room. They each found a chair or table to sit on. The last through the door were Jerry Mays and Vince Reedbanks. Doug and Jerry had arrived a week ahead of the rest of 15802, and had called this meeting of the senior technical crew to debrief them of what they had learned so far. Doug turned and stretched his arms out on the window sill behind him.

'So here we are, chaps, the Ides of March,' said Doug.

'You saying we should beware, sir?' asked Corporal Muir in his sharp Ontario twang.

'No, corporal, but be alert. This place is on an active footing now. We're going to be thrown into some gruelling practice routines. Day and night. We've all done field training, but now we've got to be working perfectly in sync with the air crews, even if we're on the hoof. Speed is everything, and all the kit has to work. You had better make sure you know how to fix anything'.

'That's a change. We were told when we first landed in England to stick to our own jobs' said Muir.

'Correct, it's going to be different now. Where we'll be going might not have easy access to spare parts. This stuff has to work wherever we are. The CO has been very clear what we are about here.' Doug looked around the room, 'where's Corporal Firby?' 'He said he had something to attend to sir' said one of the other Canadians. 'Did he? We'll have to see about that.'

They went through the expected routine for the coming week and the men dispersed, leaving the three officers together. The three men hadn't been together for some months, since the dance at Deeping in fact. While Doug was at Langtoft, Jerry had spent time at Northstead. Vince Reedbanks had been posted to Church Fenton ahead of the other two in January to help set up the whole operation. It looked as if he was heading for promotion to squadron leader.

'What was that?' asked Vince.

'That was a soiree,' said Doug, the annoyance in his own voice annoyed him intensely, 'what do you think it was?'

'You could have told me about it, I only got wind of it from Muir on his way here. I've been here a good bit longer than you, and know the ropes a damn sight better...'

'...and we've got to know these men better than you,' interrupted Doug, 'so it made sense to call them in. Didn't know where you were, actually.'

'In the Ops Room, where I always am in the morning'

Jerry interjected at this point. 'Chaps, keep it civil. Look, Vince, we're just working this lot out. The crew have been a bit jumpy, and there are a few characters we have to keep onside.' 'Like bloody Firby,' muttered Doug. 'Sometimes these Canadians get a bit above themselves. Only just arrived with the team and started bad mouthing the officers. And I bet you haven't been dealing with a lot of that since you got here.'

'Well, haven't you just come up in the world?' said Vince.

Doug shrugged and walked out.

'What is up with him?' asked Vince

'Look, I reckon he's a bit lovesick. He was supposed to see Eleanor at the weekend before coming up here. She never turned up - sent him a note to say her friend at Skegness was taken ill and she had to head over there,' explained Jerry.

'He shouldn't take it out on us.'

'In fairness, Vince, I think it's only you. He hasn't forgotten Market Deeping, I reckon.'

'What's that got to do with anything?'

'Use your imagination. The man's in love.'

Doug slouched his way back to the equipment shed, a hangar being used to house the heavy equipment of the mobile radar units. There would be an exercise tomorrow and he needed to be sure everything had made it from Hibaldstow. He felt his earlier behaviour was bordering on petulance, and he was giving himself a good mental kicking for reacting in the way he did. But he had to admit to himself that he was struggling. He wanted to fly, he wanted the men to be easy, he desperately wanted to see Eleanor, and he really thought Vince had been assigned to another signals unit. He seemed unprepared for this whole adventure.

It wasn't just Market Deeping. In fact it wasn't even Market Deeping. He knew all the men fell in love with Eleanor at first sight. They couldn't help it. No, Vince's ham-fisted manoeuvring hadn't bothered him, but his omissions had. The summer of '43 had been a pivotal moment when Doug had finally understood he had duties and responsibilities to those around him. This wasn't a military thing, except he acknowledged this might have had a part in it. As a pilot he thought he was always considering the safety of his crew, but in reality he flew planes for himself. For his own sense of achievement, for the adrenaline, and to show his older brother he could do something too. While they had been close, Doug had always felt something of a follower. He followed his brother into the local youth football team, into the scouts, into some apple thieving (which didn't end well). He had followed his brother into technical college to study engineering, but that had been interrupted by the outbreak of war. First James was called up, joining the Royal Artillery, and he eventually followed into the RAF. That was a conscious decision. He felt the Army was too prosaic, hard work and in the front line. Not that he felt afraid, but he had a curious feeling that being up in the air gave him more control, more command over events below him. Up there one could see a bigger picture. Besides, going to the cinema when he was growing up he remembered vividly the images of airmen standing by their planes, cracking a bottle of beer, and generally looking like it was all one big party. Doug liked parties. And then there was his mother. He finally felt a sense of responsibility to her. He had never given it a thought before. She was 'there', always available, often chiding, but constant. Ever since his father died when he was eight years old, she was all the authority and guidance he ever knew. She adored her sons, and he had taken it for granted. She knew there was nothing she could do about the call-up, but she nevertheless begged both of her sons to find roles in the armed forces well away from enemy fire. Disappointment on both counts.

So in that summer of '43, Doug met a woman he could not stop thinking about, and he began to understand his own vulnerability, to emotions and bullets alike. This gave him an insight into how others might be feeling. This illumination of empathy was something of an epiphany, and brought with it a new and heavy burden of responsibility. He was mortal, and so were those he loved. How had this escaped him? In August that summer he had taken some leave to visit his mother in Paignton. It had been eight months since his last visit, and he vowed to up the frequency. The other change that summer was that Doug acquired a dog, a border collie called Pup that had belonged to an injured pilot from a fighter squadron at RAF Syerston. The two had struck up an early friendship, and the dog had taken to Doug immediately. When the pilot's plane crashed in a training exercise he was badly injured. He had asked

Doug to look after the beast in just such an event, because the ground operations had a better chance of seeing it through the war. He wanted the dog to have a secure home.

Doug took the dog with him on the trip home, calling loudly to his mother as he opened the front gate and walked up the garden path towards the casually left-open front door. 'Mother, darling! I've brought a new friend to meet you!' He let the dog off the lead, and it went to make itself at home among the rose bushes, briefly returning to say hello to the beaming woman emerging from the house, before heading back towards the undergrowth. Mother and son embraced and exchanged observations about the nature of canine character and behaviours before going through the door. Doug babbled away as if he had returned from a morning stroll to the shop and back, rather than an eight-month separation. His mother was mostly silent, soaking up the tide of small talk that flowed around her and once more filled the silent corners of her house. She was desperate not to smother him, but equally desperate to wring out every ounce of affection and pour it into him, to nourish and protect him as she always had. Her life was a rather solitary affair now, and she greatly looked forward to her sons' visits whenever they could get leave. In James's case this was never, since he went to North Africa, but at least Doug was on home shores, and on the ground.

Doug's father had been injured in the last war, being returned home in 1917. He had been on the periphery of a gas attack, and his troop had failed to be warned about the deadly breeze drifting across from the epicentre. While he had managed to get his mask on, his exposure had been severe enough to put him out action for the duration, and he was repatriated. His recovery was strong at first. Married and working life resumed, and Doug was born in October 1918. His father, however, succumbed to influenza the following year, a patient of the pandemic. This weakened his compromised lungs still further, and while he survived he was susceptible to heavy chest infections every year. In the autumn of 1926 he developed a cough that turned into pneumonia following a long wet walk over Exmoor designed to build up his stamina. He died on Doug's eighth birthday.

Deirdre Highcroft had married at seventeen, with her first child arriving just before her eighteenth birthday. She was twenty-one when Doug was born, and found herself to be a widow and single mother before the age of thirty. Her father had run a successful local hotel, selling up on the eve of the First World War with enough money to invest in a local building business, and to buy a house for his newlywed daughter and husband. Her marriage was something of a local event, bringing two notable families together that would probably start a new business dynasty in seaside visitors or development. But the call-up had put paid to all those notions. She survived on a war widow's pension, and a small income from helping her father in his business affairs. Doug and his brother never went without, but she found bringing up two boys on her own a stretch on her emotions, if not her finances. She poured her heart into the two children, determined that they would not suffer from the lack of having a father. Not all the local community were charitably disposed towards single parenting, and seemed to keep her on the edge of social groups. Everyone felt sympathetic for her situation, but somehow they couldn't help judge the failure of a wounded soldier, one who did not return in a box as a posthumous hero. She knew this was how they looked at her family, because she sometimes could not hide her own disappointment from herself, and the anger at her bright young man coming home to her beaten and betrayed by his line of command. She would placate herself with the thought that the failure was with the commanding officers, not him.

'So, Mother. I have two big things to tell you,' Doug announced in a rapid change in direction of the conversation. Goodness, she thought, how will I keep up with him? 'First is that I've put in for a transfer, back to my old squadron. There's an opening for Squadron Leader. I'd be flying again, Mother!' Her heart wilted a little. 'But are you fit enough, dear? Will they let you fly, aren't you a little out of practice?' She knew she sounded lame and naive. 'Nonsense, Mother, I'm fit as a fiddle. I had a full medical and physical a couple of days ago, they reckon I'm back to normal, I've been training like mad. I filed the request for transfer when I heard the old squadron leader had moved on, three weeks ago. They said all they needed was an A1 medical report and it would be considered very favourably. I left the medical report with Vince Reedbanks to pass on to Wing Command, he was heading up there anyway.' He took a deep breath, his eyes widened and he spread out his arms, 'imagine, Mother, I could be flying again in a couple of weeks!' His new-found sense of responsibility had deserted him as he once again imagined the adrenaline rush of firing up the engine of a Beau. "It's all happening, Mother. There's definitely going to be a move against the Hun soon, now the Yanks have taken charge. There's going to be some serious action, and I reckon I'll be right back in it.'

'So is that your two big bits of news, dear?' she said dryly, and turned towards the kitchen door, 'I'll make us some tea?'

'No! Wait until I tell you the most important thing. I've met the most wonderful woman. She really is the kind of girl any man would marry. Mother you would love her.' She stopped dead and turned slowly, 'Are you planning to marry her?' 'No...yes...well no, of course not. But maybe I could - one day', 'You shouldn't be marrying anyone in the middle of a war. When did you meet her? What does she do?'

Doug spent a full fifteen minutes, it seemed almost without troubling to draw much breath, explaining the party, the chance encounter, how he spent the following afternoon with her and her friends before they departed for their station in Lincolnshire. 'It's really very close. We can see each other every few weeks when our leaves coincide. It'll be more difficult when I'm back in Scorton, but I know she's the one. You'll have to meet her.'

Doug had left out a few details in his recount, which in his mind were no longer important. Events can often be significant one moment, but then merge into a fog of lost memory and lose their potency and poignancy, until they resurface to ambush a false sense of complacency.

Perhaps he was truly at ease. Where did his outward cheer and charm finish and his inner turmoil and doubt begin? It was almost impossible to tell with Doug. He seemed to never have a doubt or worry. The only clue was his self-deprecation, but even that seemed to be a confident form of irony. He always just seemed to move on to the next thing when something, or someone, tried to get in his way. That's not to say he flitted, he just kept moving, and if people came with him, well that was a huge bonus. One worthy of throwing a party. He instinctively felt his mother would encourage him on this latest emotional journey, just as he was convinced that Eleanor had already bought the ticket and jumped aboard.

'Doug, that dog of yours,' her attention had been redirected to the animal coming into the hallway with something in its mouth, 'what has he brought in?' The dog had discovered the patch of grass in front of the house smelled just right for his urgent bodily needs, which he thought worthy of presenting in person to his new host as an offering of friendship. 'Ah yes! Marvellous isn't he!'

On his return to Staythorpe, Doug had made straight for the post room. He knew it would be too soon to have a reply from Scorton, but his impatience got the better of him. There was a note waiting for him. He'd been summoned to the squadron leader's office. 'Highcroft,' said the squadron leader, 'thanks for coming by so soon. This request for transfer has been declined.' 'What, sir? Why, sir? Wasn't the medical good enough?' 'They never received any medical report, but they had already decided they needed fly-ready crew. You'd need a couple of months back in the saddle before you're combat sharp. Other applicants were better suited.' Doug had not heard the explanation, he heard - in his head only - 'Reedbanks never delivered the report....'. 'Besides,' his commanding officer was continuing, 'we've had a request from HQ to provide good officers over in Lincolnshire. Not sure which one yet, but they badly need officers with your experience.'

For the first time in his life Doug felt a blind storm raging in his head towards another human being. Bloody

Vince Reedbanks! Was this payback for being rejected by his girl? It was obvious she didn't want the man's advances because (a) she liked Doug more and (b) she didn't want to fall out with her best friend. The man was completely deluded, and now he had probably wrecked his final chance of getting back into a plane before the big offensive. He scoured the base, and ended up at Vince's billet, where the landlady met his banging on the door. No Vince wasn't there, she told him impatiently, he'd been called home three days ago as his father was very sick, possibly dying for all she knew. Bloody hell, thought Doug, as he made his way back to base, don't people know there's a war on? What's with all this need for everybody to visit sick people all of a sudden? He knew he couldn't raise any of this with Vince, the man had serious family issues that actually made his own problems insignificant. Doug buried his internal hatchet, determined not to let it see the light of day. But it was probably the main reason he applied for another transfer anyway. At least he knew where he would like to be working in Lincolnshire, which was when he put in for Langtoft.

Chapter 13

Anna in Berlin
Paignton, December 1989/Berlin, October 1982

'Berlin totally transformed my life,' said Anna. They were starting on their third bottle of wine and she felt her inhibitions leaking away. She was relaxed and ready to tell her story. She gave Jane and Molly a brief run-down of events that led to her flight from Hamburg. They sat there in disbelief, and listened transfixed as their friend related the events of the next six years.

'When we arrived in Berlin I decided I wasn't going to speak to him until I could start believing something he said. He was nervous and shifty, kept asking me what was wrong. I think it was days before I said a word.

'We went to the Schöneberg district where Aaron had a friend who lived in one of the squats. If you thought King's Cross or the King's Road were cool, they had nothing on Schöneberg. Life right on the edge, the fiercest place I'd ever seen. At first I was scared stiff. To survive there you really had to be super cool. But pretty soon I got to love it. I kind of reverted to what I knew, and managed to join a band. There were clubs everywhere. We started going to SO36 and Berghain. We were living a couple of streets from where Bowie and Iggy used to live. It was wild!

'We started hanging out with these artists and musicians. Ever heard of the band Einsturzende Neubauten? Well you should. I sang with them once. These guys practically invented Techno. It wasn't Kraftwerk that started it, it was Tangerine Dream - remember that argument we once had about whether whale song was music? Those guys just kept inventing stuff. I met them too. The scene was very young, but the city was full of crazy artist types trying to break the mould. It was an island of cultural madness surrounded by a communist state.

'I felt safe. Completely removed from the crooks who were looking for us. I doubted they would want to come into this world. But Aaron didn't feel safe at all. He was never comfortable. You remember his taste in music? No, that's because he didn't have any. It was all a front with him. That image was camouflage. He found it hard to fit in. Plus he was convinced this guy Frank would catch up with him.

'Anyway, Aaron started working behind a bar in a club in Kreuzberg, and I got some slots DJ-ing. I learned to use the desks and the kit. Here, Mol, see that tape there? Stick that on. That'll give you an idea of what I was listening to back then.

'It was a great way of life but it wasn't earning us much money. I got to understand how sound systems worked, you know, were wired up. I became a bit of a techno-geek. I found some part-time work in the local hospital helping the electrician. Before I knew it they offered me more work, and I fell into doing general maintenance. There was this engineer there said I should go to college and get some qualifications. So I did. It all just happened, there was no plan. Things were fine for a couple of years. Gigging, studying, partying, working. I felt on fire, I was really living. I never felt so good.

'And then it all went to shit. I guess I ignored the signs. Aaron wasn't happy. Actually he didn't have a creative bone in his body. He could pose a bit, but he didn't understand this world at all. We started arguing. I'd tell him he was better at stealing stuff and dealing drugs than trying to hang out with this scene. He would say he'd never go back to that life. But guess what? That's exactly what he was doing. There were loads of drugs in Berlin, and they had to get in somehow. Aaron found himself a nice little niche selling to the clubbers in Kreuzberg. I suppose I knew he was up to something, but he always denied it.

'Anyway, it turns out that many of the supply routes came into Hamburg, and happened to pass through

Hamburg to get into Berlin. Do you see a pattern here? One night we were sitting in a bar and in walks Frank. Yes, Frank the gangster from Hamburg. He came straight up to our table, stood over Aaron and started calling him every name under the sun. Snitch, thief, murdering bastard, etc etc. Well the murdering bastard bit threw me I have to say. I thought we were dead. Frank had three or four guys with him, there was no way out.

'I wasn't ready for what happened next. Aaron pulled out a gun and shot him, right in the chest. No discussion, no warning, just BAM! Fucking killed him. I'm serious.

'Well Frank's boys melted away, and some of Aaron's mates, who I didn't even know, clustered around us and started giving him advice on how to get away. We were walking down the back alleyways and I was shouting at him, asking where he got the gun, how long he'd had it? Did he know Frank was coming for him? He kept telling me to shut up, that he was thinking. 'Well that'll be a first,' I said.

'It didn't take long for the police to pick him up. He'd told me to move out and live somewhere else for a while. So I was never implicated. No-one put me at the scene, every one of his gang members denied knowing me, so when it came to trial I was never called or questioned. The police had of course pulled me in to find out what I knew, but strangely they believed the truth.

'Aaron is now in prison. Fifteen years. He pleaded self-defence, which they must have believed a bit or he would have got life. So there you are. He was just a crook with no imagination. He was a liar and a fantasist, and was forever dragging me into a dead end. Perhaps to actually be dead.

'By the end of 1984 he was inside and I was by myself again. Except now I had friends, part of a scene, and I was learning to become an engineer. I was getting an education in every way. Berlin is the coolest place on the planet, vibrant and alive. God knows what bringing the Wall down will do. I guess the money-men will move in, smarten it up and make a killing, and shove all the artists out in the cold.'

'So why did you come back?' asked Molly

'I'd had enough, ran out of steam. I was fully qualified, started a good job. But I couldn't handle the club scene any more, and couldn't keep the DJ-ing and other plates spinning. My friends were moving on, some drifting back west, others heading for New York. I looked around one day and it all felt flat. I'd had a couple of boyfriends, but nothing seemed rooted or solid. Then earlier this year I received a letter from Aaron. He wanted me to visit him, which I did. He said that on good behaviour he could be out in a couple of years, and would I wait for him?'

'What did you say?'

'I told him to fuck off. He'd deceived me too many times. And of course I realised his politics made everything impossible.'

'When did you realise that?'

'It kept niggling at me, but I pushed it away. But there's one thing that really sticks with me. One time we took a trip into East Germany. It's not something you do often because of the form filling and questions and hours of queueing, but people do – did – travel across the border a lot.

'We went to the Sachsenhausen concentration camp, which they had turned into a national memorial to the Nazi, atrocities back in the 60s. A bit rich because the Soviets and East Germans used it to keep their own political prisoners for years. It's a really gloomy place, and they have these attendants moping around the place, they seem like guards. Very unnerving. There's this huge obelisk put up by the Soviets to mark the liberation of the camp. And then there are the rows of huts where people were housed or put to work. It was a desolate place.

'It mainly housed political prisoners at the beginning of the Nazi regime. They rounded up the academics and professionals - anyone in a position to denounce them. It was a way of snuffing out dissent. I don't think they killed people to start with, just locked them away and made them work - make stuff for the Reich. Eventually they made uniforms for the Wehrmacht, you know, the army.

'They started rounding up other political prisoners and Jews, and that's when it got overcrowded. There wasn't enough raw material for everyone to work productively, and they were running low on food. So they started killing them. First they shipped out the Jews and Gypsies to the death camps, but as the war went on they would shoot them in this camp too. They recently found a grave of over 12,000 bodies.

'It's a sobering experience because you realise the Nazis never had a plan. They had no idea of where this would end up. With hindsight we think it's obvious, but it kind of crept up on them. Bad ideas end up making bad people. The prison guards didn't necessarily start out as murdering thugs, but they ended up brutalised and brutalising.

'So there we were, Aaron and I, wandering into one of the huts where the people had slept. There were wooden bunks and everything still there. It was like no-one had touched the place in 40 years. I made some remark about how it would have been a living hell and Aaron said 'some people deserve what they get.' He wandered off in a different direction. I stared after him, but he was oblivious. He didn't say anything else, and I was too puzzled to question him - we always steered clear of politics. But it never left me. I was sure from that point that he had some Nazi sympathies.

'I couldn't believe that there were still people who might think the Nazis had a point. Of course we'd seen it with the National Front. You know if we don't keep watching out for these bastards they'll creep up on us again. I kind of realised what the Second World War was all about. It wasn't all bulldogs and Blighty spirit. Our parents' generation really was fighting a war of principle, not just survival. Theirs was a sacrifice for a way of life. Sorry to get heavy, but I had a moment in that camp that revealed something I never understood before.

'Anyway, this was just before he shot Frank, so everything came at once. I was done with him after that.'

'Why didn't you call us when you got back?'

'Because I thought you'd be pissed off with me. I'd dropped you, everyone. I got back to London feeling like a complete failure. I'd burned every bridge. I'd been as selfish as Aaron. It had all been about me, and I felt I should have given something back. And now there's no-one to give it back to.'

'There's us,' the other two said in unison.

'You've already started with this music,' said Molly nodding at the tape machine, 'it's fucking brilliant!'

'So, changing the subject,' said Jane, 'who was that mystery man at the crematorium?'

'I have no idea. It was the same man I spoke to in the pub a few weeks back, the ghost I told you about.'

Anna had to explain the 'ghost' story to Molly, about how she had no idea who he was or how he had found her.

'Well there was a guy.' said Molly

'What guy?'

'Some old guy, some months after you'd left. He came asking questions around the Cross. I met him in the Skinners. I have to say he looked out of place in there. You know, a bit too smart for Judd Street. He said he was looking for you, had something to tell you. I told him I didn't know where you were. Probably in Hamburg. I told him that you'd be with a guy called Aaron. He was very insistent to learn as much as he could. That was it really. I never saw him again.

'Hey,' said Molly after a moment's reflection, 'you don't suppose there's a link between me talking to this guy and Frank tracking you down?'

'I really doubt it Mol,' said Anna, 'Aaron was probably a shining beacon who was easy to find. The fact that he was carrying a gun tells me he was expecting trouble. This guy, did you tell him anything else about me?'

'That we'd been in a band together, that you'd lived up in Islington.'

'Could be that this was enough for him to find out all that stuff about me. And did he say his name?'

'Yes he did. I think it was Harry.'

□

Chapter 14

Portland Harbour, 4th June 1944

It was cold, with squally rain being driven across Portland Harbour by a strengthening wind. Ft Lt Richard Hurrell, Medical Officer, lay on netting strung across the back of a transport lorry, the canvas roof providing shelter from the rain. He was grateful for the warm clothing he had borrowed, and was now focusing his attention on staving off the seasickness that he knew would envelop him as soon as they left harbour. He had been on board his landing craft since yesterday morning, and the weather had deteriorated that afternoon. The day before men had been swimming in the harbour, but today was one of boredom and sombre reflection. It was 4.30 in the afternoon and he was anticipating the starting of the landing craft engines. He was hungry, but unable to eat. A fear of sickness, and a deeper sickness of fear for where he was going. 'I don't belong here,' he thought, 'I should be with Paddy. Where is she now? Did she get my message?' Hurrell had been plucked from his honeymoon two days before, with orders to report to his new unit at Portland harbour. He had been assigned to GCI 15082 at the end of May as their Medical Officer, but he remained with his flying squadron while he requested emergency leave to get married. He and Paddy had planned for the wedding to be in June, but he had convinced her that with the invasion of France imminent, he would much rather be a married man heading into the fray. She was inwardly reluctant, but she knew it would give him something to cling to. Besides, she thought, he had assured her he would be among the last to land, after the troops had cleared the way. Medical staff were always better sheltered. He didn't tell her that the call five days after his wedding had informed him he would be in the advance party. He would be part of the first wave of the invasion.

It was a strange kind of honeymoon. They spent the nights together at the local coaching inn, and he travelled back to his camp at Ibsley each morning. One day he didn't return. He had been given his orders on the Friday afternoon, put on a transport lorry, and suddenly he was headed for certain doom. He tried to get a message to Paddy, but wasn't sure if it had been delivered. And now there was no way to contact her. He spent that first night in the cabin of the truck, dehydrated and stiff having spent a couple of hours drinking and philosophising about war with the driver. They had sat by the roadside with a bottle of gin in a long convoy queue heading into Portland. 'I may never see England again,' he ruminated. 'Well it won't be England if we don't go and beat them up,' growled the driver. 'I just want to know how we let this happen. In fact I want to know how the Germans let this happen. We had one bloody awful war, and they go and start another one.' 'Good for your trade, Doc.' 'No it isn't. Waste of time and talent. We should be making lives better, not patching them up.'

He was woefully underprepared. He had managed to borrow some warm clothing from one of his new comrades, Duggie (or was it Doug?) when he arrived. A man so full of positive spirit that Richard almost forgot they were going into war - it felt more like some scouting adventure with Doug.

When Hurrell first caught sight of the harbour he thought he'd been brought to the wrong place. Where was his new unit? He had gingerly stepped down from the cab, muscles and head aching, and stared in disbelief across the harbour. He could barely see water. Landing craft crammed so close together that one could walk from one side of the harbour to the other. It looked like this was going to be his new quarters, maybe his last. And with the evening temperature dropping he had no warm clothing. He was miserable at the prospect of a cold night in cramped conditions, and certain that the next day he would be sent to his doom. He must have looked like an abandoned puppy, because a voice came at him over his shoulder.

'You must be the new Doc. You look thoroughly miserable, old man.' Doug introduced himself.

'Hello, Richard Hurrell. Good to meet you. I'm a bit disorientated. Was pulled away from my honeymoon. No chance to properly say goodbye to my wife.'

'Where's your kit?'

'Just this bag. No time to pack. I was told the unit would have everything I needed.'

'Here,' said Doug, rummaging in his kit bag, 'I've a spare pullover and scarf. Hang on to them. I think the weather's on the turn. Gets cool out on the water at night.'

He spent the next hour or so with Doug introducing him to his new comrades. It almost had a party feel to the whole thing. He briefly met the wing commander, who gave him the briefest outline of their role in Hitler's certain downfall. At least he felt he had purpose. But it was something Doug had said stayed with him, which had started to pull him out of his introspection and self-pity:

'Just imagine if these Nazi bastards get to be in charge. Can you? No, of course you can't. We take it for granted that the world we know will just carry on. Even in the middle of all this shit. It's real, this war. This is the fight we have to win. The alternative would be too terrible to live with. Do or die and all that. And if we die those behind will just have to bloody well fight harder. There isn't any other option.' It wasn't all breeze and jollity with Doug apparently.

Any lingering optimism had been dashed by his first meeting with the Padre. Squadron Leader Geoffrey Fordham and Richard found themselves standing on a transport truck roof, leaning on the side of the landing craft and looking out over the crowded flotilla of ships and craft. Each man instinctively recognised the other as a fellow outsider, both having specific functions, albeit for different aspects of the men's well-being. The Padre was the older of the two by some eight years, and while he was only eight years old at the outbreak of the Great War he had vivid memories of the news reports of the day, and later his father's recounting of his time in the trenches. Hurrell's own father had been a medic in the trenches of Flanders, and had also recounted to his son grim stories of why war was to be avoided at all costs. The conversation soon fell to what lay before them.

'Tell me, Padre, does your faith give you any greater courage for going into battle?'

'In truth have no idea, since I have never been without my faith. Moreover I've never been into battle, so this is a new situation for both myself and God. He has never tested me before. But I believe I will not have much time to be talking with Him. I hope that my focus will be on the support I can give to those around me. I have no idea what form that needs to take. And you? What will get you through this ordeal? Your role in all this is at least well-defined.'

'I won't lie to you, I am petrified. I am sure I will not get out of this alive. The Germans have been dug in for years, and we're planning to float up onto a small patch of sand and ask them to move on. How are we prepared enough? The weather's closing in, most of the men haven't met each other before, and we don't know what we're supposed to do when we get there.'

'Well, just because you're new to the unit doesn't mean that others are not so well acquainted. I've noticed some very strong bonds in this outfit, and all you need to do is count on the man next to you. But let's be clear, this will be no seaside picnic. Men will die. Some will have a life-changing experience, like my poor father. But our job will be to respond to whatever we find on the ground. You came with good credentials, by the way. I heard that you had saved a man's life in training. I am sure you will live up to your professional calling.'

'Thank you, Padre. I'm not a bad medic, actually I think I'm quite good. But I'd make a poor soldier. And I can't find any sign of a God to give me a helping hand.'

'Then be a medic and not a soldier on that beach. And leave God to me. He's going to have to answer to a few things when this whole debacle is over.'

'Well the mortal command here will also have something to answer for. I have only one medical orderly. I'm not sure how we'll cope.'

Richard felt humbled. The Padre hadn't preached at him, but expressed a faith in his abilities. He thought he had done nothing but complain since he had left camp, and already he had met two inspirational men. Although perhaps that was because of the desperation he felt constantly rising in him. His spirits lifted a notch, but he knew they had a long way to go before he could return this level of kindness these men had shown. And now as the engines were fired up at last he remembered what his WAAF friend had said a couple of weeks ago. 'You won't even be needed' she said, 'once Jerry realises we're finally coming for him he'll pack up and head back to Berlin'. He hoped it might be true, but he didn't really believe it. No, this felt like the real thing, and they were about to be carried to certain destruction.

GCI 15082 were housed on five landing craft, with about 150 men and their equipment. They would provide guidance support for the air cover once the bridgehead had been established. The five GCI units were being spread across the entire landing force. That previous evening they had learned they were landing with the Americans on a beach codenamed Omaha. 'We'll have been pounding it for hours before we arrive, they'll be nicely softened up by the time we land,' the Wing Commander had told them. 'These Yanks don't like surprises, so we'll be in good hands.' When asked if there would be any British troops in support they were told that all of their compatriots were further down the coast. Everyone was equally prepared, and it made no difference where they were going to land. Their designated landing point would be at the quiet end of the beach - it would have been cleared by the time they even got sight of it.

The flotilla moved out of Portland harbour late afternoon surrounded by deep gloom. They moved parallel to the coast, but never made it past the Isle of Wight. The wind was getting stronger and the waves higher. It was lashing with rain by the time the fleet was turned around and heading back to Portland harbour. The landing craft were not designed for rough conditions, and many of the trucks were shifting around. Even seasoned sailors were sick. Hurrell surprised himself by keeping his stomach contents in place - not that there was much to hold down. He was mighty relieved to be back in harbour, hoping the whole show would be postponed, or better still abandoned. But they had to spend that night surrounded by the smell of vomit and an intensifying sense of apprehension.

The next morning the Padre called an impromptu service. He stood on top of a truck and tried as best he could to project his voice across the cluster of craft that constituted his immediate flock. His sermon was not designed to be one of false hope. Rather one of realism. Tell it as it is. Encourage each man to look out for his comrades. Do not fear death or injury. Only be afraid of fear itself. This was what Hurrell had been telling himself throughout the build up. Would he be consumed by fear and try to run and hide? How would he react in a real battle? Nothing, he thought, had prepared him, or any of these men, for what they were about to encounter. After the service the men resumed their aimless wandering around, playing cards, and the odd practical joke. There seemed to be a small change in the mood from feckless restlessness to determined resignation. The Padre considered he had done a reasonable job, particularly when Hurrell visited him from the adjacent boat and congratulated him on his efforts. 'I haven't heard the CO provide any inspiration, but you gave them a common sense of what needs to be done there.'

***

5pm that evening, 5th June 1944, they set sail again. The clouds had lifted a little and the rain had stopped. They were told the wind had dropped, but no-one believed this. The sea seemed as lumpy as before. And this time as they saw the Isle of Wight recede behind them they knew this trip was the real thing. Under any other circumstances anyone looking out over the advancing armada would have marvelled at the scale of the adventure, and the sheer audacity of the ambition. Each landing craft seemed to be fighting its own battle with the waves, the engines periodically straining and over-revving as the vessel pitched and rolled. After a while the men on board got used to the asymmetric rhythm; they used it to mark time passing and guessing the distance travelled. Many concentrated on listening for sounds between and beyond the noise of their own boats, in particular any sound from above. Everyone had expected the enemy to be bombarding them with everything the Luftwaffe had. But there was nothing. The clouds in the sky did not appear to be hiding vast squadrons of aircraft ready to blow holes in their sides. There was a vague optimism that the RAF had been doing a fine job of containing the foe. The very air out here seemed to be British. But the mood stayed subdued for the most part.

Jerry Mays made his way through the vehicles heading to the front of the landing craft. He had picked up Hurrell on the way, who he found lying on his netting staring at the roof of the truck. He was sure the medic had been muttering something, but he gave the hammock a shake and goaded him on to the deck. 'Come and join the lads up front.' There was considerable noise and laughter from the forward vehicles.

'Bloody hell, Doug, can't you give it rest for a minute?' It was Vince Reedbanks, who sounded more irritated than usual at Doug's constant stream of banter. Jerry wondered if Vince was just miserable, or did he reserve a special resentment for the fact that Doug was able to attract and hold the attention of a group around him. 'I'm sorry. old man, but you have to admit it's a bit absurd – ahh, Jerry! Doc! You've decided to join the fun!' Doug was lighting a cigarette. 'I was telling the lads about a fishing trip I made out here a few years ago. This very spot. Weather was beautiful, the sea was calm, and we filled the floor of the boat with mackerel - even pulled out a couple of cod.' 'So what was so funny?' asked Hurrell. 'The Flight Lieutenant here was speculating on how we could make a fishing line out of the netting,' said Vince, 'and catch us something decent to eat.' Oh food, please no, Hurrell inwardly groaned to himself. 'But it's what he was suggesting we could use as bait. You don't want to know.' chipped in Corporal Firby.

'What?' "Oh seriously, you don't want to know. I'd leave it be - you look real queasy as it is.'

Someone produced a deck of cards and suggested a game of pontoon, with matches as chips. They agreed they would settle up with a redistribution of rations when things were settled at the other end. The value of a matchstick being assigned to various items of ration allowance. No-one could see what settled might look like in their mind's eye, but at least it gave them a future to hang on to.

Reedbanks and Hurrell sat out of the game, watching from the corner of the truck. The banter continued unabated as the game proceeded. Hurrell wasn't convinced there was a real game going on. It reminded him of the card games he'd play with friends as a child, no-one paying attention to the rules or who was winning, although the loser tended to be treated mercilessly as a failure of human endeavour.

'What's with you and Doug?' asked Hurrell.

'Nothing. He can be relentless at times. He doesn't pick up on the mood around him.'

'I'd say he does rather - he seems to be lifting a few spirits around here.'

'Personally I think he's playing to himself more than others. He could be more honest, that's all.'

'Do I sense some tension?'

'We've had our moments. I think he blames me for the fact he's here at all. He asked me to take the results of his medical to HQ for his application for re-assignment. I wasn't able to do it - unavoidably detained you might say - and needless to say he didn't get transferred, and it's all my fault. Except it isn't.'

'Oh?'

'They weren't going to let him fly again anyway. He'd been grounded too long. He's got to stop blaming others. This is all a front. Frankly.'

'Have you two talked about this? I mean just as you're heading into the front line shouldn't you be patching things up?'

'Look, I trust the man. Professionally he's top notch, and I don't doubt he'd stand by anyone in trouble. But I don't have to like everything about him. When this is over I doubt we'll be pals. We have a different view of the world.'

Vince also held a suspicion that Doug was jealous. Vince's promotion to squadron leader happened shortly after Doug had been passed over. He had to admit that their relationship had been a continual round of challenges, always due to circumstances beyond their control. He didn't want the animosity, but it kept creeping up on him.

As daylight faded they were advised to try to get some sleep. They would arrive at the French coast around dawn. They planned to land mid-morning, and, in the words of Wing Commander Anderson, 'You all want to be fresh and ready to face the enemy.' Not that they were expected to see the enemy. They had learned that the plan was for the first wave of American troops to land at low tide at daybreak. The naval guns would have silenced the German artillery, and the ground troops would attack the dug-in positions, and clear the beach of obstacles for the second wave. By the time they landed they would wander up the beach, and set up the radar equipment to guide in the air support. They would hardly know there was a war on.

☐

Chapter 15

Anna and the Lord
London, December 1990

Anna and her friends had stayed in Paignton for a couple of days, spending the time to get properly reacquainted. Their friendships, they discovered, were built on more than punk adrenaline and posing. They had shared some formative times together, and they were still touchstones of empathy for each other in an otherwise contingent world. Anna felt hugely unburdened at having shared her story. More than this, she knew her friends had welcomed her back into their lives, now that she had let them into hers.

When Anna returned to London there was a letter waiting for her. It was on official House of Lords headed paper and titled from the office of Baron Jervis of Greenwich, and was hand written. She looked first at the signature which simply said, Howard.

Dear Anna (if I may)
When my personal assistant told me that you called, and the nature of your enquiry, I felt compelled to write to you in person. It does appear that you have links to my time in the war, and your surname is indeed one that I recognise very well. I would very much welcome meeting with you to discuss your family background. I hope that I can shed some light on your research. But I have to say that I am more than a little curious about the connection. Hence this personal note. May I suggest that you call my office again to arrange a suitable time to visit. My personal assistant has a much better command of my diary than do I.
Yours sincerely

Howard

She was astounded. A lord of the realm writing to her in person. These people were easier to get hold of than she had imagined. She started to feel nervous. What would she say to him? More importantly, what was he likely to tell her? When she called his office they set a date for the second week in January. She would have to get through the holiday period on tenterhooks. She called the agency and asked if the hospital wanted her to work over Christmas and New Year. She had no other plans and it would serve as a distraction. Besides, the money would be good seeing as how she had had all this time off.

On Christmas Eve the hospital maintenance crew finished early and went the Crown and Anchor pub behind Euston Station. The narrow bar was crowded and noisy. People had brought in a portion of the outside damp and the atmosphere was thick with humidity and smoke. Anna, Bert and Mo squeezed into a section of ledge by the window. Somehow Mo had managed to find a stool, 'Your round, Bert,' he shouted. Bert made the usual huffing and puffing noises, but he was always the first to put his hand in his pocket when he got to a bar. The crowds seemed to part effortlessly as he made it known he was 'coming through'. When he returned 10 minutes later with three pints in his hands, a cigarette protruding beyond his drooping moustache, and a look of great concentration on his face, Mo said, 'See, the mountain comes to Mo!'

'Give it a rest, Morris, you prize plonker.'

Mo and Anna had been talking about how one of the contractors had royally screwed up that day, and how it had been touch and go whether they'd get the medical gases back on for the afternoon theatre lists. Mo had a BIG OPINION about this, but then he had big opinions about most things. The conversation could have carried on all night if he wasn't steered off it.

'Listen, Anna,' said Bert,' I was really sorry to hear about your mother. How was the funeral?'

'Thanks, Bert. It was quiet. Just me and a couple of friends. Mum didn't have anyone else really.' She was starting to feel a bit emotional, which took her by surprise.

'To tell you the truth it's been much tougher than I thought it would be. I told you I was trying to find out more about my dad, well it's all got a bit weird.'

'Parents are all weird,' said Mo, 'did I tell you about how my dad used to go AWOL for weeks on end?' He had, but the other two ignored him.

'How so?' said Bert, keeping his gaze on Anna.

'I found stuff that connects them back in the war. I even went to the old RAF base, where I met someone who knew my dad. I've got a picture of him, too. But something's missing. And then there's Harry.'

She didn't want to be having this conversation, but she couldn't help herself. Mo would probably tell the world about it, but Bert radiated an empathy that made her open up. His eyes were wide and looked at her intently.

'Who's Harry?' he asked.

'I don't know. But I think I've met him. He knew my mother before I was born. He seems to have been in love with her. He found me in a bar in King's Cross a couple of months ago. He really spooked me, called himself my 'ghost'. And he came to my mum's funeral. Crept in at the back and ran out as soon as I saw him. He just disappeared.'

'Woooooaaaaahhhh!' said Mo, raising his arms in the air like some spectre from a 1930s horror film.

'Mo, can you ever be serious for one minute? Would you ever just fuck off?'

'Well it is all a bit spooky like you say. A ghost at a funeral. You've got to admit it's a bit classic.'

She turned to Bert with a sigh.

'What did he say to you? In the pub, I mean?' asked Bert

'He started by telling me what I had been up to for the last few years. He didn't know much, but he had tracked me down to King's Cross in the early 80s, then to Hamburg and on to Berlin. He must have been to those places because he knew the street names, clubs and bars. But he didn't know any of the details of my life, but I got the feeling he could picture me in those places.' She finished her drink. 'Morris, your round. I'll have a gin and tonic. Large one.'

'What! This is just getting interesting!'

'Get the drinks, Mo, or we'll all die of thirst here,' said Bert. Mo slid off his stool and wormed his way into the crowd. 'Go on.'

'So then he started talking about my mum, asking me when I last saw her, and what did I know about her. I didn't want to tell him very much, I thought he might go and bother her or something. But he started to talk about her mental health and whether I thought she was completely stable, and I told him it was none of his business. He shrugged at that.

'But then he asked me what I knew about my father. I told him he died before I could know him. That he had a good war record, so my mum always said, and he was the kindest and funniest man she'd ever met. She never forgot their time together in the war and couldn't believe her luck when she ran into him again all those years later, and when he needed a friend. This man, Harry I now think his name is, kind of snorted at that. And then he said the strangest thing - "I strongly suggest you look up your father's war record. You've spent all these years not knowing much about him, so my advice to you, as a friend - and I am a friend - is to find out about him for yourself. You might start by asking your mother to be more forthcoming about him, but you will need to investigate the man for yourself."'

'I can't ask my mother anything now, but I am finding some clues. And here's another mindblower, I'm going to see Lord Jervis in a couple of weeks. He used to be Minister for the Arts, you know. Turns out he was commanding officer in charge of both my parents. He's agreed to meet me!'

'Blimey you have been busy. Good for you.'

Mo returned from the bar with the drinks.

'What's that about a lord? You turning religious or something?'

'Sometimes I despair,' said Bert. 'Here, let's go to that Bhel Puri restaurant down the road later.'

'No,' said Mo, 'let's go to the curry house next door to it, I fancy a vindaloo.'

'I always despair,' muttered Anna to herself.

***

Baron Jervis of Greenwich had an office that was tucked away behind a row of committee rooms on the first floor of the Palace of Westminster. She was met at St James's Gate by an assistant who led her through the main lobby between the two houses of legislature, and up a winding staircase. The slightly faded feel of the place surprised her. The building felt like it was in real need of repair. Perhaps she'd try and get a job here.

When she was led into his office, Lord Jervis was sitting in an armchair and he invited her to sit opposite him.

'Will you have some tea?'

'Err, yes please. Thank you for seeing me - Lord Jervis.'

'Anna, it's a pleasure to meet you. Please call me Howard. I think first we might start with you telling me a little about yourself. And why you have chosen now to look into your family past.'

She had expected this, and had decided to limit what she would tell him. She had no intention of mentioning the ghost, or even the name Harry. She wanted to focus on her mother and father. She gave a potted history of her childhood, and the little she understood of her father's background, and the story she knew about her parents' relationship. How it was the death of her mother that sparked the need to discover more about him. While this was true, she was aware it was only part of the story. But if she told him the full truth, then he would ask more about her life in Germany, and she would probably tell him too much. It was better to steer clear of tricky territory.

'I looked up my old records of the people at Langtoft, and there was indeed an Alison Gardner. But I have to say I don't remember her very well, if at all, to be frank. She may not have been there all that long. Some of the girls were moved around to fill the gaps where they were needed. But Doug Highcroft. I do remember him very well indeed. He was a real character. He came to us late in 1943, and was transferred the following February.

'But, my dear, can you tell me more about how your mother met him. Later I mean, after the war.'

'All I know is that they met again at the sailing club in Paignton. Apparently he had moved back to be with his mother after his first marriage failed. That's all she ever said.'

'Well it's true that he was from that part of the world.' He was measuring his words, and looking at her with a rather doubtful look.

'But I found something recently that bothered me. My mother changed her name by Deed Poll in the months before I was born. I never found a marriage certificate, or his death certificate for that matter. In fact I can't find any record of his death whatsoever. But I keep hearing stories about him. He seemed to have been a very memorable sort of guy.'

'Yes, he was. Tell me, did your mother talk about his first wife at all?'

'No, but I found this photo.' She passed it over. 'I'm sure he was having some sort of affair with that woman.

'Yes, that's Eleanor. They were madly in love.'

'So where did my mother feature in his life? Was he the kind to have several woman on the go at once?

'No. It wasn't like that. Relationships between the male officers and the ACWs was frowned upon. It was only because Doug had flying and battle experience that this relationship went unchallenged. Doug and Eleanor met before he arrived at Langtoft.'

'Can you tell me more about him? What he was like, what he did in the war. Did he marry this - Eleanor?'

'Doug Highcroft, the man who's name you have, was one of the most amusing and spirited men I have ever met. When he arrived at Langtoft in November of '43 he was always bubbling with energy, but underneath ran some deep frustrations. He had been a night fighter pilot in a Beaufighter squadron. His plane was badly shot up, and he received a serious injury to his leg which grounded him. Even when he joined us he was convinced that he would fly again. He did often say he felt he wasn't contributing to the war effort and wanted to do more.

'One time at a shindig in a local pub an RAF pilot came in, very drunk, and started bad mouthing all of us ground officers. Wingless wonders he called us. Said we had no balls and were just pretending to fight a war. Well that riled Doug no end - all of us really. There was a nasty feeling in the air, but then Doug took him down with the most amazing blast of sarcasm I have ever heard. He wasn't a violent man at all, but wanted to speak up for the honour of his fellow radar crew. It was brilliant.'

Howard Jervis fell silent. He was gazing at the floor, lost in a memory moment.

'You know I have been having this idea of writing a play, a radio play probably, about our experiences in the war. 'Wingless Wonders' would be rather a good title, don't you think?'

'Who would listen to it? I mean who would the audience be?' Anna was surprising herself. Here she was asking a peer of the realm about her family history, and now questioning his ideas. And instead of pulling back she pressed him a little further, as she realised she had a genuine sense of enquiry. 'Wouldn't it just be a bit of nostalgia? Like Dad's Army.'

He chuckled a little. 'I take your point. But no, it would need to speak across the generations. It's true that we lived through an intense few years. It defined many of us, probably all of us to some extent. But we didn't choose it, and we were subjected to some of the greatest miseries a human being can endure. We can't let that happen again. You know, I sometimes wonder if the difference between our two generations is the greatest generational divide in history.'

'Why is that?

'Well there's the culture for one thing. As Minister for the Arts I did have plenty of opportunity to reflect how much things have changed. But then I think that's all relative. Every century sees big cultural shifts. I think it's more than that. We didn't have the freedom to follow our desires. We were compelled to do our duty. All our lives were on hold due to the call of war. And we did it, if not gladly, then with a sense that the world would be better for our sacrifice. And so it has proved to be. Peace in Europe, greater prosperity for our children. Education, health, freedom of expression are all possible because we defeated the fascists - people who would have suppressed all that is inquisitive and creative. But I worry for the future, for your generation.'

'In what way? Isn't everything getting safer now? The Berlin Wall has come down, Germany can reunite. The Russians are talking to the Americans. They say the Cold War is over.'

'Well, maybe. As you may know I was heavily involved in the Campaign for Nuclear Disarmament. I'm the first person to celebrate the coming-together of a fractured Europe. But that doesn't change the fact that all those weapons are still pointing at each other. We've a long way to go to remove that ever-present danger. But that isn't what I'm trying to say.

'By the time your generation reaches my age I think you will have forgotten how you got here, how your freedom was won, and how it is maintained. It's more fragile than you might think. We won't be around to remind you, short of endless repeats of Dad's Army, which I'm sure people will get tired of. And you will feel guilty that you had so much, on the back of the hardships we had to endure. My fear is that you will want to redefine yourselves, appropriate our experiences and want to believe that you endured it too. You will want to own the British bulldog spirit, and cast yourself as Churchillian clones.'

'That's rubbish. No-one I know thinks like that. Everyone wants peace.'

'I hope so, but it is all about context. I don't believe human nature changes down the generations. And yours is the wealthiest, best-educated, with access to more entertainment and exposure to more diverse cultures. I don't know if you will be able to use all of this richness of culture and learning to truly understand its value. The true value of peace.'

'We don't live in some utopia you know! Not everyone has the wealth and education you talk about. There are millions of poor and deprived people. Right here. And they're as pissed off as ever. I thought you were a socialist.' Whoa, Anna, she thought.

'Yes, I am, and of course you are right. And maybe that's where the fault lines will open up. The capitalists may well overreach themselves with their greed, and be too complacent to see the trouble coming. We are witnessing the reunification of a country 45 years after it tore itself in two. I predict Germany will be one country within a year, and it will take decades to properly heal the rift. Other countries in future may do the same self-harm. History tells us that it only takes a disturbance in the system big enough to stir up deep discontent. So, Anna, what I ask of you is this - please will you be vigilant, you and your brothers and sisters, to make sure the dark forces don't rise again.'

'I don't know if that's possible. We're only just able to look out for ourselves. What is the Bible passage? Don't attempt to take a speck out of your brother's eye when you have a bloody great plank in your own.'

'I'm not sure it says it in those words, but I take your point. All I'm saying is don't sleepwalk into disaster, as we did in the 1930s. We need to peel the blinkers from the people - the ones that the Tories and the bankers have put there for their own rewards. I worry that we are being carried on a tide of complacency. Make no mistake that the tide will go out on our golden age of liberal freedom. If we leave people behind, or freeze them out, the next incoming tide will not be so forgiving.'

'You're an old communist really, aren't you?'

'Oh no! Stalin's pact with Hitler put paid to that. It's true I was thrown out of government for being too left wing. But I don't see being against nuclear weapons, and wanting a more equal society is a danger to the state. On the contrary, it would be the making of it. It's essential.'

Anna was troubled by the way the conversation had gone. While she had lived a turbulent life of her own, it came with some certainties. Politicians lied, rich people controlled the powerful, and most people struggled to have enough to be comfortable. But she had been able to express herself, educate herself, and change her life for the better. And now this man was challenging the fabric of society, a fabric that had been invisible to her, until now. She wanted to return to the purpose of her visit. She no longer worried that being direct might be misconstrued as rudeness.

'You're evading my questions, though. I had hoped you would tell me more about my parents. What did happen to my father?'

'I am going to give you some information, and then suggest you follow it up yourself. You have been doing a very good job so far on uncovering your past. Doug was transferred from our station to GCI 15082 in March '44. It was a mobile ground control unit that was set up as part of the Second Tactical Airforce. All part of Operation Overlord. The preparations for the invasion of Europe - D-Day. 15082 was one of a number of RAF radar units that would go ashore on D-Day to guide the fighter cover for the invasion. Doug volunteered when he realised this was his last chance to see action. I think he finally accepted he wasn't going to pilot a fighter plane again. I had volunteered too, but Doug got in ahead of me. Plus I think he had already worked with some of the other co-opted officers in the unit.

'So, my dear, go and research GCI 15082. There will be a good many records. And when you have found out all you can come and see me again. I will fill in whatever blanks I can. Meanwhile I will endeavour to find out more about your mother. I have some ideas about who to ask for information about her.'

Anna could see that he would not be pressed further. She was getting used to people telling her to go and find out about herself. But if they knew stuff why didn't they just tell her?

'Thank you,' she said, 'I appreciate you seeing me. I'm sure I'll be back to see you.'

'Not at all, anytime. I think what you are doing is highly laudable. Do not hesitate to call me.'

They stood and shook hands. He squeezed her hand in both of his and smiled warmly, wishing her well in her investigation, but he still had a slightly wistful and distant look in his eyes.

***

She sat with a number of documents and folders set out on the table in front of her. The large open-plan area seemed over-lit, and the room was too warm and the air dry. Several other people were similarly stationed around the room at identical tables, heads bowed either in reading or scribbling notes. The young man on the opposite side of the table to her had a large cellular mobile phone sitting on the desk next to him, which his hand kept moving to. It was around the size of a house brick cut in half lengthways, with an arial poking out of the top. She wondered why he needed such a thing, and why he kept having to look at it every couple of minutes. As soon as she had settled and found her concentration the machine made a loud beeping sound, which elicited an excited and jumpy response from the man, who seemed to yell into the thing. The records office staff were immediately on him 'Take that outside please!' He walked out of the room still, it seemed, trying to understand what the person on the other end was saying to him.

The Public Record Office in Kew was now a familiar place to Anna, and she understood how to look for material. She was returning this time with a precise knowledge of what she was looking for. The assistant who brought out the files had made a comment that one day she would be able to read this stuff in her own home. There was a plan to scan all the national archives and store them in a large mainframe computer. 'The world wide web is going to allow us to read anything, anywhere,' the girl had said. Anna wasn't sure what she meant by that, although the hospital had recently set her up with an email account that she could use to contact some suppliers.

Now she had recovered her concentration from the disruption of the man's phone, she opened the operations record for Base Defence Sector 21. She had managed to establish that GCI 15082 was part of BDS 21, which in turn had been set up under 85 Group. While she didn't understand all of these structures she had a document with names, places and dates. At first glance the BDS 21 operations record ran from January 1944 to late October that year. At the beginning it contained lists of personnel and equipment, and various location changes of the different units. Sure enough, there was GCI 15082 based at RAF Church Fenton. In the middle the records became more detailed, and she soon realised they were personal reports of individuals in the run up to D-Day, and then D-Day itself.

She started reading line by line from the start, but it was too procedural and dry, and she soon started fast scanning the pages for names. She found who she was looking for first mentioned in March '44 - Flt/Lt D C Highcroft transferred to GCI 15082, Church Fenton. She skipped forward to the run up to D-Day. Entries from a number of individuals started to paint a picture of life ahead of an impending battle. There were entries from, among others, the commanding officer, a padre, and the diary of the medical officer for 15082. These entries from 1st June onwards became more detailed and caught her attention, and she became immersed in the story that unfolded. She realised that she knew nothing about what happened on the Normandy beaches, and here were first-hand accounts. She read, head in hands, consumed by the words as they came off the page. She was confounded by the horrors that these men were writing about and yet the seemingly objective account that they provided. In times of war, it seemed, people can only present an honest and straightforward account of their experiences; there was little room for analysing and philosophising, that came later.

When she finished reading through to about the middle of June '44 she sat back with her arms folded, staring at the pages in front of her. She didn't move for five minutes, before she turned back the pages to 6th June, and started reading them over again.

☐

Chapter 16

Omaha Beach, 6 June 1944

Dawn did not so much break as emerge. The greyness of the day before persisted. Those men that didn't wake with the light were soon roused by the stirrings of others. There was a rustle of restless activity in the landing craft. They were a couple of miles from the shore, unmolested by gun fire or attack from the air. Some of the men had slept well, others had lain awake all night still marking the sound of the engines. The relentless movement of the waves was a deep cause of unease and sickness, for those who had tried to eat anything. There was a good deal of talk about wanting to be on land - how it would be better to be fighting on terra firma than waiting around in this vomit tub.

Suddenly they could hear the guns open up. The landings had begun. It was a remote spectacle, impossible to make out at this distance. Anyone peering above the side of the LCT had momentary glimpses as they rose and fell in the waves. They could see craft lined up and stacked deep looking more like an oil slick, waiting to unload their cargo of weapons and destruction on an unremitting enemy. The bright patch of sand darkened with the swarms of men and armoured vehicles seeping across the beach like an ink stain. But individual movements were impossible to distinguish. No-one could tell how the action was playing out.

There was nothing to do but wait. No card games or smutty banter would distract any man from his reflection, apprehension, or suppression of demons. They were to land at 11 am, so they had some hours to kill. At the allotted hour the GCI craft, together with a third wave of American marines, started to move in, only to turn around within minutes. New orders had arrived to pull them back.

It was four in the afternoon before the group moved again, this time running all the way up to the sand. The tide was on the way out, exposing the obstructions on the beach that had supposed to be cleared by the first wave of engineers. Even before the landing craft doors were lowered they were keenly aware of the sound of heavy gunfire. The battle was not over. They were not about to stroll onto secured and cleared beaches.

Doug was in the second vehicle off his landing craft. The water level immediately rose half way up the cabin, water pouring into the footwell. The engine sputtered, but kept going. There was enough traction to pull the truck out of its trench and onto flat sand. Doug glanced to his left - from the adjacent craft the first truck wasn't so lucky. The landing craft had beached on a sandbar, and the vehicle sank below the water, with strong breakers tilting it sideways as it went. The crew managed to scramble out and started swimming for the shore. It struck Doug that this wasn't the part of the beach they were supposed to be on. They had been promised an easy route off a practically non fortified section, but here they were among the defences and in range of an 88mm gun that was picking targets along the beach at regular intervals.

Doug saw that Vince Reedbanks's truck in front had made it beyond the water line, but had got tangled in some razor wire, and its progress was stopped. Meanwhile, he had opened the cabin door, and was pulling a couple of men from the water. He saw more trucks driving into deep water, this time heavy equipment vehicles, all sunk, with the specialist gear on board that they were there to set up. He watched their purpose for being here disappear in front of his eyes. But there was no time to think. That 88mm was finding new range at the water's edge, and they had to get clear of the beach. The driver steered a course to the left of Reedbanks's truck, but soon saw there would be no way through the barricades. There were some burned out trucks further up the beach, probably from the first wave - these would be their best bet for initial cover, but there was a distance to cross to get there. Doug knew they needed to clear a path up the beach. He saw that Vince had had the same idea, he had dropped down from his cab and with two other men was trying to cut the wire and break up the barricades with a sledge hammer, making painfully slow progress, like running in a dream. The bursts of machine gun fire didn't seem to be in their direction.

As Doug weighed up the options he looked at the beach in front of him properly for the first time. What he had taken for heaps of debris, rags and general detritus of war were in fact corpses. More than he could have imagined. The horror swept over him as he understood that probably the entire first wave of American troops, and most of the second wave, had been wiped out. They hadn't managed to breach the defences at all. Some of the gun placements were silent, so they must have achieved something, but this battle had been raging all day, with line after line of infantry slaughtered before they could reach dry land. And beyond all of this he saw American army vehicles queued up at the beach exits. Even if they made it through the defences there was no way off. He felt physically sick, this was not what their training had readied them for. Focus, he thought, let's get off this beach. At which point he heard shouting behind him, he thought it was Firby. 'Sir, we have a problem back here'.

Jerry Mays and Richard Hurrell were in the last vehicle off the LCT. As soon as the rear wheels dropped off the ramp the LCT skipper threw the engines into full reverse throttle pulling the craft back. Jerry knew this was to make way for the landing craft behind, but he couldn't help thinking there was some undue haste in the skipper's retreat. 'Which way, sir? There's no route forward,' shouted the driver. 'Go left,' said Jerry, 'there's an opening 100 yards down there.' Ahead of him he saw their convoy had formed an untidy crocodile up the beach. The open sand to their left was due to the vehicles in the adjacent LCT never making it to land - all sunk with their crews now desperately swimming for solid ground. 'Stop! We've got to help these chaps to safety. And some of these vehicles might be salvageable. Get word up the line that we'll need help back here.' The next while was given over to getting men and equipment to shore. It was evident that these men, sea sick and laden with gear, were quickly exhausted by their efforts, and some were being carried away down the beach by the strong currents.

Hurrell took off with three others to get help. He had made it halfway along the line of vehicles when the first shell hit. It was rogue, and some way off to his right and behind him, but it had the distance of the rear end of their convoy. He was sure that soon they were going to need medical assistance back there. The one medical orderly in this unit was up front, so they were spread very thin on the ground. It wasn't supposed to be like this, he thought. Why didn't those damn commanders listen to him when he complained about the shortage of orderlies? Did they give a toss about the welfare of these men? But he knew he had to recruit help for the men at the water's edge. The second shell landed in the water, close to the ramp of a newly arrived LCT, disgorging its contents into the line of fire. Men tumbled off into the rising sea as one truck was blown sideways. 'Get the casualties ashore,' Hurrell yelled, 'bring them up the beach'. He kept running to the front of the convoy where he found Vince Reedbanks and Wing Commander Anderson organising the attempts to break up the barricades.

He called to Vince, 'We're going to need people back there', another shell landed, this time closer to the back of the convoy, 'and we're going to have to set up a casualty station up here'.

'Give me a minute to finish this off and I'll come back. Find Doug, he was behind us.'

Hurrell ran around the truck to the easterly side of the convoy. Strangely he felt more protected here, the beach ahead eerily empty, except for casualties of the earlier waves. He found Doug inspecting the back of his truck. 'Bloody broken axle. Must've happened when we dropped into that trench out there.' 'I need your help, Doug. There will be wounded coming up here soon, and we need to set up a station. Have you seen Reid, my MO?' Together they set out to organise the transfer of casualties, and try to get some order into the chaos.

'Look, Doug, there's a load of foxholes in the line of shingle up there, should be safe from the worst of the shelling, and good cover from the machine guns. Let's get casualties taken up there.'

'Looks like they're already taken. American soldiers probably.'

They ran the thirty yards up the beach to the first shell hole. Inside were two American soldiers, badly wounded but alive. The medic set to work on them and instructed Doug to find Reid and get the message down the line where to bring casualties.

***

Squadron Leader Fordham, the padre, found himself 100 yards further east of the rest of 15082. They were driving across to join the broken crocodile when the shelling started. He was looking for the advanced beach party that would show them where to go, but it was soon apparent that no party existed, and no vehicles were able to leave the beach. A queue of wrecked and abandoned US troop carriers clustered at the two nearest exits. A couple of ruined tanks lay broken on the top of the dunes. When they arrived at the main group the rescue operation was in full swing, and he joined in. He understood the orders were to wait for instructions and get the GCI units off the beach in an orderly fashion - but there was no order here. He instinctively felt he had to get all these men to the top of the beach. The artillery was picking them off at the back - the only way was forward.

He found Corporal Firby running back from the front of the line of trucks. "Corporal, where's the Wing Commander?'

'He's been running between the GCI groups sir. We're scattered along to the west there, and he wants to get them over here. I heard he'd been hit sir, but he's still running around.'

Padre took a decision, with an injured CO and no guidance from the advanced party someone had to find a way out. He looked to his right at the blocked beach exit. It was a bank of earth filling a shallow gully, surrounded by abandoned vehicles. But it was the one calm spot on the beach. No troops, no target practice, certainly no shelling. 'Come with me, Firby, and bring those two men over there.'

They ran up the beach, across the shingle line, dropping into shell holes and dug-out foxholes on the way. Some of these shelters contained the bodies of American soldiers. It seemed lying down was as dangerous as running around upright. They kept moving as fast as they could. On reaching the earth bank it was clearly a hastily made obstruction, one that could easily be removed with the right earth-moving equipment. Why hadn't it been shifted before? Surely the whole American wave hadn't been cut down? There would be more tanks and vehicles on the beach here, they must have moved off somewhere else. Padre climbed up the earth bank to see a small group of houses on the other side. They were intact and looked unscathed by the bombardments from sea and air. He beckoned to the other men to follow him to the first house. As they approached they were astonished to see three German soldiers run out of the front door, and over to the house behind. Well that's encouraging, he thought. Maybe we can get the men to shelter up here. More of us will probably get those Germans to move off still further, they look as shell-shocked as those Americans down there.

Padre and Firby went back to the beach, leaving their comrades behind to guard the house. As if by a miracle the first thing Padre noticed as he surveyed the beach was a bulldozer. Where did that come from? It must have just landed, but he couldn't make out which LCT it might have sprung from. 'Firby, get over to that bulldozer, direct it over here. I need to get the attention of the rest of our unit.' He realised he'd have to head back into the fray to broadcast his plan. He vaguely felt he was technically committing mutiny, but he knew he had no alternative. He had to save lives.

***

Doug and the Doc had made some progress with the makeshift field hospital. At least there was a place to bring the wounded and fly a red cross. But most of Hurrell's work was on the hoof. Many of the injured needed immediate attention - bandages, tourniquets, morphine. The shelling was now moving up the line. A single 88 mm Flak gun could fire several rounds per minute, and had a high degree of accuracy. Presumably spotters in the cliff tops were directing the fire up the line of the broken convoy. It was systematic, and while each truck provided a semblance of shelter there was really nowhere to hide. The two officers, who had only made each other's acquaintance two days earlier, now worked as a pair moving towards the sea checking the state of the injured as they were being brought along the line. Those deemed safe to move were transported on to the 'hospital', those in dire need administered morphine, and maybe a patch to hold them together.

They bumped into Wing Commander Anderson. 'You're hurt, sir,' said Hurrell. 'Arm got knocked against a lorry in a blast - bit sore, think it might be broken. Gash on the leg too, but I'm fine.' Hurrell convinced him to at least bandage the leg, and offered him a sling for the arm - duly refused. They then saw Jerry Mays about three vehicles ahead of them. He was tending to an injured man, tying up a bandage. A shell exploded on the far side of the truck forcing Jerry to go to ground. There was a sharp cry from the other side of the truck, which Jerry instinctively responded to by jumping to his feet and scurrying around the other side. Vince Reedbanks lay in an awkward heap, his left leg twisted up behind him. There was no foot attached to it. It lay, like some carelessly discarded boot, under the truck. Next to him was another man, unconscious with a head wound pouring blood on to the sand.

'Jesus Christ, Vince!' He didn't have any more words to say. He found himself struck dumb from that moment. He reached in his medical kit for a bandage and started to apply a tourniquet, at which point Doug and the Doc arrived at his side. "You're going to need morphine, old chap,' said Hurrell, who worked fast and efficiently to deliver the injection. 'Jerry, I want you to put a bandage over the wound, nice and tight - I need to see to this other chap over here, he looks in a bad way. Doug, help me move him clear of this wheel.'

Vince was still trying to sit up, having hoisted himself on to an elbow to see the state he was in. He glanced at Doug who said, 'lie down Vince, we'll have you out of here and get you all fixed up.'

As they turned to the other man, another shell landed next to them. Life is a devilishly difficult thing to extinguish. From the murderer's panic that they might not finish the job, to the inheritor's frustration waiting for the last gasp, or even the uninitiated first attempts at wringing a pigeon's neck, there are many witnesses to the tenacity of a living being. Even in extreme conditions it seems the body can be immortal, and has some unbreakable tether to the circadian rhythms of light and dark. But mankind has invented ever new ways of delivering catastrophic trauma, and ensuring the job can be quick and complete.

When the shell hit they all fell flat in a huddle, and felt the blast and shower of sand that covered them with a searing abrasion. Hurrell and Jerry lifted themselves off the ground, but Doug didn't. He whispered 'they've got me, Jerry.' Hurrell gave him a shot of morphine and said, 'finish Vince's bandage will you, Jerry?' before turning to bandage the other man's head wound. When they turned back to Doug, he was dead.

'He was never going to make it,' said Hurrell, 'his lungs were completely shot away.'

'My God,' said Jerry, 'Oh my good God'. He was aware that the only words he'd spoken in the last few minutes had all invoked some religious symbols, and he himself had always thought of himself as immune to religion. He stared at his dead friend. He was vaguely aware that Vince Reedbanks was grabbing his forearm, pulling at him. 'What's happened, what's happened?' he was gasping, but the mixture of morphine and shock was making him weak and he fell back in a swoon. Jerry continued to stare, kneeling and with one hand now clutching his hair, as if to pull himself back into the here and now. Hurrell was shaking him.

'Jerry. Jerry, listen to me. We have to get these injured men up the beach. Now!'

☐

Chapter 17

Clubs and swastikas - Anna and the Lord - Part 2

London, February 1990

Howard Jervis was already seated at the table in the restaurant. She saw him and indicated to the maitre d' that she was expected.

'Thank you for coming, Anna,' said Howard, rising from his chair as she approached.

'Thank you for inviting me.' She was looking around her at the rather grand surroundings of the club restaurant. She felt underdressed and a little self-conscious; she had never been inside anywhere like this before.

'Oh, you are very welcome. I'm afraid I have put you through something of an ordeal, and felt offering lunch was the least I could do.'

She had called his office after her revelatory trip to the records office. She had left a message that she had discovered the truth about Doug Highcroft, and now she was more confused than ever. Could she come and see him again? He had written back immediately with this invitation to his Mayfair club.

'It's a little grand for a socialist politician isn't it?' she said, and immediately regretted it, 'sorry, sorry, I didn't mean to be rude.'

'You're right, it is. And I confess to feeling somewhat guilty, but you know the machinations of government revolve around places like this. Conversations happen out of the way of the watchful gaze of Fleet Street. So I became a member of a couple of clubs.

'You know my wife once berated me, towards the end of the war, for requesting an overseas posting. She thought I'd sold my soul to the capitalist military machine, and just wanted to prop up the system. It wasn't very revolutionary of me, of course, but I did want to see some real action before the whole thing finished. But maybe she was right. How do we balance radical change with the need to influence from a position of power? Someone has to get inside the system.'

'I suppose,' she said, 'I'm afraid my entire rebellion has been shouting anarchist lyrics, or joining the local subculture.'

'Subculture is hugely important and shouldn't be underestimated. It's where tomorrow's mainstream is born. In my time as Minister for the Arts I saw a great deal of talented youngsters who deserved a bigger platform. I always tried to promote ways of giving it to them, but by and large they made it on their own merits and pure determination. The arts are tremendously conservative and hate change, as much as anything else, I suppose. Look at this new group of artists out of Goldsmiths, that fellow Hirst, for example. Can't say I like or understand his work, but from what I've seen he has a drive that's going to disrupt to whole art scene.'

'I read something about him. Not sure he sounds that genuine to me.'

'Well we could debate the place of the genuine in art, but I know you want to talk about something quite different today. Tell me what you found out.'

She paused, looking up at the ceiling, gathering her thoughts and trying to find the best way to approach it. Direct would be best, she thought.

'Doug Highcroft died on Omaha Beach on D-Day. He's buried in Normandy. He wasn't my father. But you knew that, didn't you?'

'Yes I did. But I felt you had to learn it for yourself. You had already uncovered so much about your past that it only seemed right that you finished the job. I believe it will help you come to terms with it better.'

'I'm not sure I can ever come to terms with it. My mother lied. Worse than that, she built an entire fabrication of a life, and never thought it was wrong to keep me believing it. She can't have had much respect for me, or even cared much about me.'

'You are angry. Rightly so. But perhaps she was protecting you.'

'From what?'

'Let's start with who your mother was. What she was like.'

'She was often depressed and withdrawn. Sometimes she was completely disengaged from me. I suppose I was her carer, but we started arguing more and I needed my freedom. So I left her. I was too young to know what was going on.'

'I did learn a few more facts about her.'

Anna put down her wine glass and looked at him. She had been wrapped in her own cocoon of indignation that made the world around her fuzzy and remote. But these words pulled her back. She understood that she would learn something new that might have a material effect on her life. 'Go on.'

'She was at Langtoft for a short while. She joined us just before Doug. She was young, maybe 18 or 19. But it seems she joined us from RAF Scorton, where she had been after her initial training. The interesting thing is that Doug was at Scorton when he was a pilot. That's where he was injured and grounded. It's possible that they had met before.'

'Do you think they had an affair?'

'I suppose it is possible, but as I told you before he was in a relationship with another woman. They were in love and were planning to marry. She, Eleanor, told me that. The station was too small for too many secrets, and she would have known if Doug was carrying on with someone else. So I very much doubt it.

'Your mother left us in January 1944, shortly after Doug had applied for his transfer to GCI. She went to a base in Norfolk, probably saw the war out there. Can I venture an opinion?'

'Yes, go ahead.'

'For some reason your mother changed her name to Highcroft, and used his name to provide you with your father's back story. I'll come to the reasons why in a moment. But why Doug? Well he was charismatic and handsome, and drew people into his orbit. I think your mother was a little infatuated with him, probably from when she heard about the injured pilot at Scorton. But when she saw that he was in a serious relationship she withdrew, especially when she learned he was going on active duty.'

'She must have known he had died. Why did she use his name all those years later?'

'Yes, my guess is that she followed his movements, and learned that he had died. It's likely the news would have got to her through the WAAF networks. I believe some of the men in 15082 ended up in Norfolk, so she could have learned it that way.'

'You said you knew the reasons why she did this?'

'No, I don't know anything for certain. But there is more.'

'Yes?'

'A man came to see me last week. Called himself Harry Drayton.'

Anna dropped her fork, which landed with a clatter on her plate. Everyone in the restaurant turned to the source of the noise.

'I see that registered,' said Howard.

'Harry,' she said. 'Did he talk about me?'

'Yes, it was mostly about you as a matter of fact.'

'This man seems to be stalking me. I think he's been following me for years. He even told me he was a ghost.'

'Yes, he said you had met.'

'Why did he come and see you? What's it got to do with you?'

'He does appear to be tracking your movements. He knows I was your mother's commanding officer in the war, so he kind of followed the same trail as you. And it led to me. And he told me something very enlightening. I think you might already know what that is.'

'Call me thick, but I'm afraid I have no idea.' This wasn't true, she was expecting what she heard next.

'Anna, my dear, Harry Drayton is your father.'

***

There was a time in Berlin when Anna had been supremely happy. One night in particular seemed to embody how good life could be. She had been at college all day, where for the first time she thought she understood what differential equations were all about. It was like she had cracked a code that only a few people had access to. A light had switched on in her brain that shone new insights into a world she never knew existed. Not that she could tell anyone about it, neither Aaron nor any of their friends would understand or care very much. It was too abstract, but it was hers, she owned this insight, and it was invigorating.

She was DJ-ing that night at a club in Schoneberg. She went back to her flat to freshen up. There was no sign of Aaron, but that wasn't unusual; they often found each other in one of their local bars during the evening. She figured he would show up at the gig later. Her set wasn't until midnight, so after she had showered and changed she put a stack of records into her back pack and headed out to eat at a nearby cafe. There she met a girlfriend, and they shared some food and had a couple of beers together. Anna was still floating on the revelations of the day, and looking forward to cooking up a storm that evening. She was buzzing.

When she got to the club it was already full and jumping. The house DJ seemed to have got the mood just right, and even though it was early the dance floor was full. She felt the thrill of the bass drum thumping into her chest. By the time she got to take over the desks, she was pumping with energy. She hadn't planned her set, but in the short time since she entered the club she had a track list in her head that would easily last the next couple of hours. She'd decided to hit them from the start, she felt they were warmed up enough to get straight in - no slow burn tonight. The crowd erupted when this first number hit its stride. She was under way, and never let up the pace for two hours. In that time she was truly elated. No drugs necessary. There was a symbiosis with the dancers - she knew what they wanted, and they trusted her to deliver. She didn't need to think about it, no intellectualising, no analysing, just raw emotional reaction to the dynamics and heavy beat of the new electronica taking this city by storm. And she was at the heart of it.

At 2 am she handed over to the next DJ, who looked at her with amazement. He had to follow that and keep the crowd going, which would be a challenge. As she stepped off the stage she saw Aaron coming towards her. 'Hey, Anna, that was really great. You're the best DJ in Berlin!'

'Take it easy, Aaron, but yeah, that was pretty fucking good.' She knew that her mood would crash at some point, but now she needed a drink. 'Come on, Aaron,' she shouted above the music, 'buy me vodka!'

A couple of hours later they were walking home. The streets were quiet, but Schöneberg never felt like it was asleep. Bars were still open, small clubs seeped music on to the streets, and it always seemed restless. They turned into their street where they saw a graffiti artist working on their tenement wall. There was a mash-up of images on this wall, which was changing all the time. But something caught their attention. The artist was agitated and working fast, but then would stop and take a cloth to the wall as if trying to rub off the image he was painting. As they passed him he turned and spoke. He sounded angry.

'These bastards. We can't have this shit in our neighbourhood.'

Anna noticed that he was spraying over another image, and then smearing the paint as if to obliterate the image below. Then she realised what he was covering up - a swastika. It wasn't a quickly daubed mark either, it had been elaborately painted using black, white and red paint, using a 3-D effect to make it stand out. This man was trying to erase the symbol.

'Who did that?' she asked.

'I have no idea, but if I find him I'll make sure he never comes around here again. This community won't tolerate fascists. It was put here tonight. I'm going to keep watching this place to see if he comes back. You keep a watch out for these people too, we can't let them be among us.'

Anna found herself shocked. She hadn't seen any fascist graffiti in this city before. There had been some in

Hamburg and other towns, but not here. She wondered what drove people to it.

Looking back on that night, with hindsight she realised Aaron never said a word to the artist, and they never said another word to each other about it afterwards. But they were a little drunk, and soon had other things on their mind when they got home.

Now, walking away from Lord Jervis's club, this one night in Berlin came back to her with raging force. A car had driven past her, darkened windows, and a house track playing a full blast; the bass pushing at the windows and shaking the street as it went. The adrenaline had been filling her bloodstream since Howard's announcement about her father, and there was a sense of euphoria she couldn't explain. Together the beat and the adrenaline triggered the emotions of that night in Berlin, and transported her to its beating heart. She thought she should be angry, furious. But the opposite had happened; she was floating again, above the melee of the street life around her. She had a fleeting sense of control over her own life that she hadn't had since Aaron had pulled that big stunt of his.

But fleeting things flee, and it wasn't long before new emotions arrived, new thoughts and new questions. Did she want to see this man Harry Drayton? She struggled to think of him as her father. Was her identity compromised? If her name was that of a dead man who never knew her, should she keep it? And, looming over all of this, what had made her mother act in the way she did, and did it matter?

It mattered. Perhaps all these questions came down to a simple explanation, but she had no idea how to look for it. Finding out who the characters in her history were seemed the easy bit. The next part of the journey looked harder, with no obvious starting points.

There was one – Harry. But she didn't know where he was, or have a clue how to find him. Given his track record of involvement in her life, and his lack of transparency when he did see her, she wasn't convinced he would be any help. If she was sure of one thing, it was that he had failed her and her mother. He was furtive and elusive. She now understood the letter she had found under the mattress. He was the father of an unborn child, the result of an adulterous affair with her mother. But she couldn't understand why her mother had to invent a fictitious father, why she didn't admit she made a mistake and decided to bring up a child on her own. Anna thought she would have respected her mother more for that honesty. 'Oh, Mum, why didn't you tell me?' she said softly. She felt herself sinking.

☐

Chapter 18

Fitzrovia encounter

Autumn, 1953

Thursday evening at 6 pm, the busiest time of the week. Alison was used to this now, opening the pub doors at 5:30 to a waiting cluster of office and retail workers keen to wash away the drudgery of another working day. It was mostly men, but there were always a few shop girls and secretaries to brighten up the dull grey suits. The business types didn't tend to frequent on a Friday, a time to go home to their families, fashion some pretence of familial solidity. She had seen what went on among these groups. They might have been bored with their jobs, but they never stopped talking about them, even while the budding affairs grew and evolved, the smell of sex and passion pervading through the thick smoky atmosphere.

Not that the Fitzroy Tavern was devoid of colourful characters. Dylan Thomas used to fall off his bar stool here with regularity. Augustus John claimed it was 'the Clapham Junction of the world'. One frustrated patron was credited with throwing the first dart to rest in the timbers above his head, which started the now famous tradition of throwing parcels of money that stuck on the ceiling. Ingrid Bergman was one of the famous names to take part in the fun back before the war. Alison was herself learning to master the art. Charlie, the landlord, was even letting her teach the customers how to parcel up the change with some bottle-top cork, wrapped in coloured paper and a dart pushed through it, and hurl it upwards with the right amount of force.

She hadn't been working here very long, and her journey to this point had been convoluted, disjointed and isolating. Since being demobbed from the WAAF she had struggled to settle to anything, and found herself moving jobs and locations frequently. From RAF Hopton she had moved down the road to Great Yarmouth, where it was thought the seasonal work would be plentiful, as people celebrated the end of the war and started to take seaside breaks again. But times remained hard and the trade didn't live up to expectations. She even worked on the docks, unloading fishing boats, until the men started returning from overseas, looking to get their jobs back. Assorted work in bars and waiting at table took her from town to town, with a trail of unsuccessful relationships. She eventually moved to London with another girl she thought of as a good friend, until she disappeared into the East End with a man she had met. A couple of years as a seamstress ended when she was 'let go' due to too many absences.

This particular Thursday was about to change her life completely. She scudded around the bar, moving from public bar to saloon and snug. Being a compartmentalised pub meant different types of people congregated in the different rooms, but in the central bar she could keep an eye on everything that was going on. A man she had never seen before eased up to the counter of the public bar, leaning both elbows on it eager to get her attention. He was tall, early 30s, with light brown hair showing under his trilby. The suit was light grey, sharply cut, more expensive than the usual in the public bar.

'A pint of your best bitter, please,' he called, seemingly oblivious to any others that had been waiting. He was ultra-confident, with a simple air of someone who expected attention. She gave it to him. As she pulled his pint he leant further over the bar.

'What's all this on the ceiling?' he asked.

'Pennies from heaven,' she said, 'customers put their change into packets and throw them up there. The money's used to take kids out on holiday. It's famous.'

'Never heard of it, I'm not from around here. Can I have a go?'

'Yes, sure. I can show you how, but give me a while for the rush to settle down.'

When the bar melee had calmed down she went back to him with the accoutrements, and asked him how much money he wanted to put in. He pulled out a ten shilling note. 'Will this do?' he asked. 'Blimey, I should say so. It's normally just the change from two bob that goes up there.' 'Well, it's for a good cause.'

She was impressed in spite of herself. She would normally be wary of flash newcomers splashing money around, but she was drawn to this man. She shouted behind her, 'Charlie, we've got a thrower here!' Charlie, the landlord, came around the bar, beaming, 'Go on then girl, show him how it's done.' Turning to the man he said, 'Now normally we'd have a fanfare, big blast from the piano, but it's a bit early for Reg to be here, so we'll make do.'

'QUIET EVERYONE,' Charlie bellowed, 'Concentration needed for this kind gentleman to find his mark!'

She placed a cork pad in the centre of a piece of red paper, added the note and folded the paper in the way she'd been taught (Charlie was very particular about this), and carefully pushed the dart through the little parcel.

'Now, you can throw it however you like, but underarm usually works best. Try to pick a bit of bare wood, or you'll hit coins and it'll bounce off.'

He took the paper dart, looked up to choose his spot and chucked it upwards hoping for the best. It stuck, and a great cheer went up around the bar. He came back to the bar as the general murmur returned and people went back to their conversations. He leant across the bar again.

'Thank you, that was fun. Look, I'd like to show my appreciation properly, what time do you get off?'

'Oh, me, I'm here till midnight by the time we've cleared up. Another night perhaps. Annie's back tomorrow – she's the real governor here, so I could get some time off.' She was worried to seem over-eager.

'I have to get back to Exeter tomorrow. But I'll be back next week. Looks like I'll have some regular business up here.'

'Exeter,' she said, 'I grew up down the way in Paignton.'

'Oh? Family still there?'

'My Dad. My mother passed away during the war. Cancer.'

'Do you visit him regularly?'

'No I don't. It's a long story. But I heard he's not very well right now.'

'Well it looks like we'll have a lot in common. How can I contact you?'

She gave him the phone number of the pub, and the times she expected to be there in the next few days. He promised to call her, just as there was a voice calling from the snug. 'How about some service over here!' 'Sorry, I've got to get back to work.' 'By the way,' he called after her, 'my name's Harry – what's yours?' 'Alison,' she called back over her shoulder.

As she crossed the bar to serve the impatient customer, she noticed two men and a woman sitting on stools by the window. This small side room had emptied out, and she hadn't noticed them before. One of the men she recognised – a local businessman who came in from time to time. But it was the woman that caught her attention. It took Alison a couple of moments to realise why she seemed familiar. Eleanor, she thought, Eleanor Durie from Market Deeping. What was she doing here?

Alison served the customer, but her head was swimming. Partly from the wave she was riding from meeting this handsome new stranger, but also seeing a face from her past, and one that gave her a deep sense of unease. At that moment Eleanor looked over, as if aware that she was being watched. Her expression changed as a realisation came across her face. She, too, recognised her former colleague. More, a former rival, and not one that she wanted to be reminded about.

Alison watched as Eleanor leaned into the businessman, older than her by a good twenty years. She touched the man's arm and said something to him as she slid off the stool. She was carrying her empty glass. He handed her some money and carried on talking to the other man. Eleanor approached the bar, never taking her eyes off Alison. 'I'd like three G&Ts please' she said, and added, 'I know you, don't I?'

'Yes, you're Eleanor Durie aren't you, from Langtoft.'

'Yes, but forgive me, I don't remember your name...oh wait... ACW Gardner?'

'Yes, it's Alison. I wasn't there very long. You were Doug's girl weren't you?'

'Yes, but that was a long time ago.'

'I did hear what happened. His friend Jerry was at Hopton with me. The news got around pretty fast. For what it's worth, I'm very sorry.'

'I seem to remember you had a bit of a thing for him yourself.'

'Well, maybe, but he chose you. I knew him when he was flying, when he got injured. But he never really noticed me. We all saw him as a real hero.'

'I don't think he died a hero's death though. Picked off on a beach with everyone pinned down. They were sitting ducks. It seems such a waste.'

'No, but Jerry did say he did what he could to save his men, look out for his friends. I can't imagine how you get over such a thing.'

'I don't know that you ever do. I was in touch with his mother. She was devastated. She said she could never forgive Germany for what happened.'

'What, blame the entire country? How can you move on?'

'I'm not sure she ever did. To be honest I don't know that I have either.'

'Forgiveness is hard.' These were words she would find herself reflecting on over and over in years to come.

'How about those drinks?'

'Yes. Who's that man you're with? I've seen him in here before.'

Eleanor bristled, and the mood turned cold. 'Not that it's your business, but he's my boss.'

'Hmm, well he's a good deal older than you. I notice what goes on in here you know.'

'Perhaps you should notice a little less.' There was no further conversation as a group of men piled in through the door, demanding instant drinks.

A while later Alison saw the businessman's picture in the paper. It was a divorce case, quite a scandal it seemed. He was the one filing for the divorce, claiming his wife was an alcoholic, and was neglecting the children. His wife claimed the man was having an affair, but there was never any evidence to prove it. Alison wondered if there was more of a story, but she wasn't going to pry.

***

After that first meeting with Harry, Alison went home to the small room she rented off Praed Street and found herself thinking about him constantly. A couple of men had shown a bit of interest in her, but Harry was different. This man looked deep into her eyes, kept his fixed on her when she talked. She felt noticed, almost interesting. The last man she had ever felt drawn to like this was Doug, the ebullient officer who lit up a room when he walked in. She had tried many times to get his attention, but it became clear he hardly noticed her, especially in his flying days. And then at Langtoft when she thought there might be a chance he was clearly in love with another woman. Alison had longed for Doug from a distance, and then accepted the disappointment when he was posted away without him saying goodbye. When she heard of his death from Jerry Mays, however, she could not shake the feeling that they had had something in common, some deep connection. She was sure he had been the man for her.

Now there was Harry. He wanted to see her again, and she wasn't about to let him go. Days went by, but no call from Harry. The next week, and then the next, came and went but still nothing. It was a full month later that Harry again showed up in the pub. He hadn't phoned ahead, but turned up as if he was walking into his local. It was early evening and the pub was quieter than usual and Alison was leaning on the counter reading the Evening Standard. She looked up and her heart jumped. She had given up on seeing this man again and had told herself to forget it. It wasn't as if they had had so much as a conversation, so she could not understand her desire to see him again. Seeing him now gave her a feeling of excitement mixed with a little resentment.

'Hello there,' he said as he walked up to the bar. 'I'm so sorry I didn't call you sooner. I got terribly caught up with work and had to skip over to Amsterdam for a while.'

'Hmm,' she said, 'and here's me thinking you might be a man to keep his word to a girl.'

'I like to think I am. So let me make it up to you. I'm in London for a few days, so how about I buy you dinner tomorrow?'

'I'm working tomorrow evening.'

'Well how about lunch then? And when is you next evening off?'

In fact they met up every day for the next three days. On his last night he had ended up staying in her room, having dodged the landlady as they snuck in from the pub. He poured all his attention on her, flattered her, bought her little gifts. She was overwhelmed and found herself in an emotional cauldron by the time she was alone again at the weekend.

He took to phoning her at the pub on her shift days, but it was always difficult to talk, and he started coming to London once a month, usually for a couple of nights at a time. She would stay with him at his hotel. He started telling her about his plans to open a London office, and that maybe he would move up. But in all that time she never knew his home address. He had given her his business address and phone number, but advised against calling it as the office was always busy. She occasionally wrote him letters, to which he never responded, although he read them because he would talk to her about them when they next met.

It was all so frustrating. No man had ever treated her so well, or had given her so much attention. She felt valued, special even. None of the other men in her life had ever been so kind. Most of them disappeared from her life, and she never knew why. She had come to the conclusion that she wasn't worth very much, was unlovable and useless, and that no one would ever want to marry her. But here was Harry who bought her clothes, took her to the theatre, and was always courteous, polite and, when they were alone, tender and attentive. She started to beg him to move to London until one day it all went wrong. He admitted to her that he had a family in Exeter – a wife and two small boys – and that he had no plans to leave her. She lost her temper badly, grabbing anything to hand in the small lodging room and hurling it at him. None of it hit him, but the commotion brought up the landlord and they were thrown out onto the street. Harry had stalked off to Paddington Station, and she was left sobbing by the side of the road. It wouldn't be the last time she saw him, but when she looked back she realised she had never again been happy after that moment.

A week after the row with Harry she received news about her father, at which point her life fell apart in every way possible.

☐

Chapter 19

Stories – Part 1

London, February 1990

The secretary sighed when she heard the pulsing pips. In the couple of seconds it took for the coin to drop and the connection to be made she imagined another crackpot caller demanding all members of the House of Lords to be rounded up and shot, or insisting the good Lord did something about the dog shit on their street. They always called from a phone box. So she wasn't entirely receptive.

'I know this is a long shot,' she heard the voice say, as she fixed her eyes impatiently on the cobweb in the corner above the door, 'but I wonder if I could speak with Lord Jervis. This is Anna Highcroft, and he did say I could call.'

'He's probably busy.'

'Well is he or isn't he? If he isn't I really would like to talk with him. It won't take long.'

Another sigh, and she noticed another cobweb in the other corner. She'd have to talk to the cleaner.

'Hello?' said Anna, 'I don't have long as I'm out of 10 pence pieces'

'One moment. Anna Highcroft you say' She put the call on hold and buzzed Howard Jervis, and still sounded annoyed when she went back to the call, 'putting you through now.'

'Anna! How good to hear from you. How can I help?' asked Howard.

'Thank you, erm, err, Howard,' she was still a little overawed to be speaking to an ex-minister of state, 'this won't take long. I wondered whether Harry had given you any contact details when you saw him.'

'Ahh. I wondered when you might ask. You were adamant last time we spoke that you wanted nothing to do with him.'

'I know, but I've been thinking. He's the only person that can tell me about my mother. And he is my father. And he has been following me. I don't think I can leave it as a loose end.'

'You are right, my dear. But I'm afraid he didn't give me any contact details.'

'So why did he come to see you? If it wasn't to try to get in touch?'

'He seemed to be fishing for information about you. Somehow he knew we were talking, and my guess is he wanted to get a message to you. Which I duly delivered.'

'That he was my father? Why didn't he tell me that the first time we met? Why go through you?'

'Yes, I agree. Very flamboyant behaviour on his part. I suggest you find out for yourself. You're good at that.' The pips went.

'Oh no,' said Anna, 'I've no more coins. I don't know how to find him.'

'My dear,' said Howard, 'if I know anything, I'm sure he will find you. Just make it easy for him.'

***

Anna sat at the bar of the Lord John Russell. It was three in the afternoon and she was on her second cup of coffee. There were two old men sitting at a table by the window, each with a half pint of stout in front of them, occasionally exchanging a few confirmatory words. At the other end of the bar was a man marking up a copy of the Racing Post, frequently rubbing his stubbled chin and chain smoking. It was calm, unthreatening, just as she liked it. But she was on edge, and kept reaching for cigarettes, before cursing her mad decision to give up last week. The man at the end of the bar wasn't helping.

She had finished reading a novel by an author that Molly had introduced her to. It was about a dystopian world in which women had been subjugated in an authoritarian and patriarchal America. It made her wonder how conditions would ever exist that people would allow such barbarity. How did this author conceive of such a world? Was she a visionary or a cynic?

Anna had pulled out her next read from her bag - Ursula K Le Guin's The Dispossessed – another of Molly's suggestions. 'A book of hope,' she had said, and Anna hoped so. She was reading the reviews inside the front cover when the pub door opened. Anna looked up. She was alert to every movement, every coming and going, every pint pulled. And here he was, at last, the man who said he was her father standing, door open, framed by a sunlit street, looking at her with a big smile on his face. He approached.

'You ran away,' she said.

'Yes I did rather. I'm very sorry about that. Not very fond of funerals'

'Not just the funeral.'

'Hmm, well that might be a point for debate. But I'm here now. It looks like you were expecting me.'

'Seeing as this is my local I'm in here a lot. But I reckoned you might show up here again. Why did you run away – at the funeral?'

'It wasn't a good time to be talking to you. I went to pay my respects to your mother.'

'Really? When did you last see her?'

'1958. Well, actually I did see her about ten years ago. From a distance you understand. I was struck by how beaten down she looked. I was worried about her.'

'And did you speak to her?'

'Didn't want to give her a shock. She didn't look much like she would cope with it.'

'I'm beginning to think if more people reached out to her she might not have been so broken.'

'I'm not sure you're in a good position to criticise.'

'No I'm not, and I'm not proud. But I'm trying to understand her now. What made her. What made me.'

Harry Drayton was silent. He looked around, as if seeking assistance or guidance on how to respond. He focused his attention on the barman and signalled him over.

'I'll have a pint of bitter, please. What about you, Anna?'

'Nothing for me, thanks.'

'Oh, come now, have a drink with your long-lost father.'

She glared at him, weighing up which of a thousand retorts she wanted to throw at him, and then surprised herself when she said, 'Fuck it, I'll have a gin and tonic. But you owe me more than a drink. You owe me an explanation. Several actually. It seems you've been following me for years. Why? And why contact me now?'

'OK, but let's sit down. That table in the corner has been vacated – a nice quiet spot.'

The two old men had finished their drinks and were heading for the door. The pub was quiet, but the audience was small and the Racing Post man didn't look like he noticed anything going on around him. The barman disappeared.

'I think it's best to start at the beginning, don't you?'

She waited.

'I met your mother on a business trip to London. She was working in a bar, the Fitzroy Tavern as it happens.' A little light went on in her head. Yes, of course, that's why she knew the history of the pub, her mother must have mentioned it when she was very young.

'But it was a while before we got together. I wasn't in London very often. But she did insist on staying over at my lodgings, and things got rather intense.'

'What business?'

'I was in print sales. There were a lot of printers around the West End back then.

'Anyway, things were on and off for a while. I'd thought about moving the business to London, and she kept badgering me about it, until I finally had to confess to her that I had a wife and two children in Devon. Yes, we were both from the same part of the world, you see. She wasn't at all pleased. Threw a vase at me, called it all off. Can't say I blamed her.'

'Very generous of you. So what then.'

'About a year later I was in London and thought I'd look her up and see how she was.'

'You're a real Sir Galahad.'

'Yes, well. Anyway, the people at the Fitzroy told me she'd had a complete breakdown, and was in a secure hospital for her own good. I went to see her. The matron there was very nice, very good to her. She told me how your mother needed some help, and if I was an old friend would I like to help get her out of there. So I said I would.'

'You get more charming by the minute.'

'Sarcasm does not become you. Do you want to hear this.'

'I think you're here to tell me as much for you as for me. Go on.'

'The matron told me what she knew of Alison's situation. It was shocking. Your mother's breakdown, it seems, had been brought on by the news of the death of her father. Not that she was sad about it – they had been estranged for years – but that it released a wave of raw emotion, a very deep hurt. It seems he had abused her as a child. She had left home as soon as she could to join the WAAF to get away from him. She'd buried the whole thing for years, but his death brought it all out.'

'Oh my God, I never knew.' Anna felt a wave of nausea run through her, and every muscle in her body seemed to go momentarily limp. A shock realisation that she never had the inkling of the forces that had shaped her mother.

'People don't generally talk about these sort of things. Especially not to their children. She never mentioned it to me, even though she knew I knew. But she let me help her. I found her a place to stay, and persuaded the pub to take her on again.'

'And you resumed the affair?'

'Well yes, but actually after a very long time. I tried several times to persuade her to move to the South West. She had inherited the family house – her mother died during the war.'

'She never talked about her either.'

'I don't think she forgave her mother for turning a blind eye. But like I say, no-one ever talked about these things.'

'I'll bet she didn't want to live in that house again,' said Anna, now wondering why her mother had gone back to it, with all its unhappy memories. 'When did she move back?'

'I don't know exactly, but my guess is when she was pregnant with you. I think that she needed to raise a child, and thought Paignton would be a better place than London. But she cut off all contact with me suddenly and without any explanation, so I only deduce this from your date of birth.'

'Hang on. You said you hadn't seen her since 1958. If she had cut you out of her life, how do you even know about me? And anyway, why did she cut you off – didn't she ask you for support or anything?'

'I'll answer the second question first. This is hard. She had had a miscarriage in early '57. It was mine, she said, and she had pleaded with me to leave my family and come and make a new life with her in London. When she lost the baby of course all such plans evaporated.'

'Of course? What does that mean? It sounds like you never even thought of supporting her.'

'It was difficult, but I did stick by her. I sent money, wrote often, came to see her when I could'

'All very distant, all very hands off.'

'Yes. But I think the second time she got pregnant was too much for her.'

'You mean she couldn't go through any more rejections. So how do you know about me? And anyway how do you know I'm your daughter at all?'

'Oh, I'm your father alright. We can do the test if you want proof. But I assure you it's true. How I know is quite…involved…if you want to hear the story.'

'I do'

'As you might imagine there was a large element of chance. When my last letter to her went unanswered, from my point of view she vanished. Later, much later, I learned she had changed her name to Highcroft and moved to Paignton.

'Interesting thing about the name you know. She once told me about a bit of a love triangle on one of the bases she was stationed at, with her and another girl competing over a dashing young flight lieutenant. The other girl won, but everyone lost, was the way she enigmatically put it. She never did speak about it again. I remembered his name because she showed me a picture of him, with that other girl. Funny thing was she told me that woman had recently married her boss – it had been in the papers. It was a curious story. But I think it's why I remembered his name so clearly – Doug Highcroft. It just stuck with me. That and the fact she carried his picture around in her handbag.'

'I know most of this already, but we're getting off track a bit.'

'Well, not really. You see it was the name that drew my attention.'

'What do you mean?'

'It was about ten years ago, no twelve. My wife had recently died. I took to having a few long weekends away, various places I always said I'd visit. I was staying in a small hotel in Weymouth, on my way to Portland Bill. It was an entry in the visitors' book, someone who had checked out the day before. Mrs A Highcroft. And then the address – Paignton. It jumped out at me. A couple of weeks later I went to Paignton, to that street – your street. And sure enough, there she was. I saw her coming out of the house.'

'But you sneaked away.'

'Look, I know this is all difficult for you, but you don't have to be so hostile. I'm trying to be helpful.'

'OK, I'm sorry. But if you didn't talk to her how do you know you're my father?'

'I did some more checking and found Alison Highcroft lived at that address with a daughter, and I found your date of birth. I knew that she had no other men in her life – she was truly in love with me – and I with her, believe me. So I knew this child was – you – were mine. And I knew I needed to find you one day. It's taken much longer than I expected. You're very elusive. Just when I think I've found you, you disappear to Germany. And when I think I've tracked you down there, you've gone again.'

'So you have been following me?'

'Yes. Who could blame me?'

Anna didn't want to respond to that one. 'Why did she change her name?'

'I don't know for sure. Perhaps it was to stop me finding her. Perhaps she wanted a cover for being a single mother – there was a huge stigma in those days.

Maybe she wanted to have a story to tell you. Maybe all of these. We'll never know for sure.'

There was a long silence as Anna absorbed the story and tried to imagine a world before she came into being, a world of people vying and tugging with each other. A cold and unconnected world with everybody looking inwards. The light in the pub changed as a late afternoon sun burst on to the street outside, reflecting off the red brick buildings opposite. It seemed to break Anna's reverie as she became aware that these February days were getting longer and that winter would soon recede. This jolt of consciousness took her by surprise, and she understood that she wasn't going to brood over these revelations. But another concern was needling her.

'You said you tracked me down to Germany. Did you go there?'

'Oh yes,' Harry brightened and leaned forward, 'that wasn't hard. An English girl with a German boy called Aaron in Hamburg. You know, if you were trying to keep under the radar you weren't doing a great job.'

'What do you mean 'under the radar'? What do you know about my life in Germany?'

'I put two and two together. I'd seen your friends in London, so I figured what circles you moved in. I was right. But just when I had your address in Hamburg I learned you had left town in a hurry. And then you did disappear rather well. It took a while to pick up the trail again. But then the damage was done, Aaron made his fatal mistake, and you were beyond my reach.'

'What are you talking about. And what do you know about Aaron's … 'mistake', as you put it?'

'Anna, my darling, when Aaron pulled that trigger, I was there.'

☐

Chapter 20

Hamburg, November 1982

Harry Drayton stepped from a bright sunny Reeperbahn into a narrow, dim lobby that led to a staircase that descended to a basement. It was early evening, the bar had just opened, and there were only a couple of drinkers sitting at the bar. He had his choice of tables. He chose a booth tucked away at the furthest end of the room from the bar, and slid in to stake his claim. The barman called to him 'Was trinken Sie?', and he indicated that he'd have a small beer. Harry looked around and felt uncomfortable. This dark cellar with a low-level throb of electronic music might be a jumping haven for late-night revellers, but right now it had the hollow melancholy of the early evening drinking den. Like so many bars around the world it smelled of spilled beer and last night's smoke, and the worn carpet had a sticky feel under foot. He was used to English pubs and European bars of course, but here he felt out of place.

He took off his tie – he didn't want to be sending the wrong signals, but it was probably too late. He was wondering if he should be here at all. When he arrived in Hamburg he felt confident that he could find his daughter easily and quickly. He had imagined how he would meet her, introduce himself, and explain how he planned to put everything right between them, and extricate her from whatever difficulties she had found herself in. He didn't know specifics but he was convinced she was in the wrong place for the wrong reasons. The little knowledge he had obtained from her friend in London wasn't very revealing, but he knew enough to be sure she was with the wrong crowd. He had one standout piece of information – that the boy she was with seemed to have two names.

He had started his search in the popular night spots, asking whether anyone had seen an English girl, early twenties, dyed black hair, probably a black leather jacket. She'd be with a local guy called Aaron, or possibly Gerhard. In one bar, near the docks, he'd been asking questions, with the usual blank looks and shrugs, when a man approached him.

'I have heard some stories of an English girl, new here, doing some work in Hamburg.'

'What kind of work?'

'Oh, this and that. Kind of work you don't want to know about. No, not that. I see you don't know what I mean. She is working for others, a different patch.'

'Where can I find her?'

'To be honest I don't know, she's not so important. We should be able to find her, but I need you to meet someone first. He will be interested to know about this Aaron or Gerhard, or whatever he calls himself.'

He gave the man the name of his hotel, and was told to go back there and wait for a call.

Now Harry sat in the booth, with torn fake leather seats and a rough varnished table top with an unpleasant patina over its surface, waiting to meet this new contact. He had no idea who or what he was going to meet. The door from the stairs opened and Harry recognised the man he'd met the day before, and who had called him last night to give him directions to this bar. He was followed in by a heavily built man wearing a white shirt, stiff unfaded jeans, and crocodile leather shoes. He had a gold chain displayed on his hairy chest. His stubble was carefully shaped, and his dark curly hair glistened from the oil that held it in shape. Harry recognised both a caricature and a man to be deeply wary of.

The first man slid into the booth seat opposite Harry, the other man unnervingly indicating to Harry to move along so that he could sit alongside him. Harry was obviously not meant to be going anywhere in a hurry. They made no attempt to get the barman's attention, and he in turn did not even seem to acknowledge their arrival.

'Herr Drayton, thank you for coming. This is Frank. His English is not so good, and neither is your German. So I will be translating for you today. We are going to ask you some questions, and if you tell us anything interesting, we will tell you something in return. Is that a good deal?'

'I suppose so. But I'm not sure what I can tell you.'

The man called Frank started to speak. Harry knew a bit of German, but Frank spoke quietly and quickly in short bursts, so Harry couldn't catch any of it.

'Frank says you should tell him all you know about this guy Aaron, or Gerhard.'

'I don't know anything. I've never seen him or know what he does or where he's from. Although I guessed he was from here – Hamburg.'

'Frank will not be satisfied with this. You know his name – names – and you know his girlfriend it seems. Start there – how do you know these things?'

Harry explained his search for his daughter, and his encounter with her friend in London.

'Where in London? How long was he there.'

'King's Cross, and I don't know – a few months I suppose.'

'Tell us about the girl, your daughter. Her name, her interests, what she looks like.'

Harry did the best he could to be convincing, that he didn't really know her, or indeed what she looked like in any detail. He assumed she was a follower of this new punk fashion and that she seemed to have played in some sort of band. He wasn't au fait with the modern world.

This was relayed to Frank whose body heaved in a single jolt of mirth before his expression became closed and deadpan. He fired something back at the other man.

'Frank doesn't much care for punks. He thinks they create anarchy. We don't like anarchy – there needs to be order. Frank prefers Whitney Houston. Now if this girl of yours is with the person we think, she should change her friends.'

'Why, who is he?'

'All I will say is this. A boy called Gerhard used to work for us. Frank thought he could be trusted, which turned out not to be true. He left us, told some lies and Frank finds himself in some trouble with the police. It's very bad to tell lies. We heard he went abroad, maybe England. We also heard he came back, with a different name, only we didn't know what it was. And he was still telling the same lies. So we think you may have helped us with this. We want to talk to him to find out why he is telling lies. So if you know where he is, you would help us some more.'

'I am looking for them myself. I don't even know this city. What do you plan to do to him?'

'That's not your concern. We want to talk to him. But my advice is this. If your daughter believes his lies, she would do well to change her mind about him. He is a bad boy.'

As the two men made to get up Frank turned to Harry and said in slow, measured English, and somewhat enigmatically 'Take good care for your daughter.' Did he mean 'of' or 'look out for' or was it a threat?

'This has been helpful' the other man said as he stood up, 'I think we will find them now. If you are at the hotel when we do, we shall let you know where the girl is.' They left.

Two days later Harry took a call from Frank's companion. They had indeed tracked the pair down, but they had left town, although he was confident that they would be found sooner or later.

***

Harry found himself in something of a quandary. He was in a city he didn't know, looking for a daughter he didn't know, and fired by a motivation he would struggle to articulate. Not that he had ever tried to explain his search to anyone. Before his wife died he gave little thought to his lost offspring. It was only after her death, after the chance event in a Portland guest house and his tentative visit to Paignton, that his interest grew. It had gradually become an obsession. He had stood on the corner of Alison's street, looking at her house, debating with himself whether to knock on the door. What would he say? What if his daughter opened the door? He was about to step into the road towards Alison's house when the door opened. Out of it emerged a person he barely recognised. Even though twenty years had passed since they had last met, Alison looked older than her years, her face lined and worried, her hair still long but mostly grey and no longer tended as it used to be. Her shoulders drooped, and every breath appeared to be a sigh. She was thin as a rake, he thought. He stepped back, and looked to retreat to the corner. He felt exposed on this quiet residential street, and wanted some cover. From a new vantage point, partially hidden behind an overgrown privet hedge, he turned to watch once more. Alison made her way to the front gate, having left the front door open, and behind her another figure stepped on to the path. She closed the door, making sure it was shut properly, before turning to follow Alison towards the pavement.

Harry was startled, and found himself rocking back on his heels, and reaching to hold on to the wall beside him. The young woman was unmistakably Alison's daughter and, at an age he guessed as eighteen or nineteen, also his own. This would be Anna – he had already learned her name from the records, but here she was, a real human being, his daughter. She was wearing drainpipe black jeans, Doc Martin boots, and a scruffy grey denim jacket. Her hair was a chestnut brown, wavy to her shoulders, shorter than her mother's used to be, but similar in the way it framed her face. He found himself immersed in a wave of conflicting emotions – guilt, fear, love. He had never expected to experience such a deep connection to someone he had never met, and only recently even knew existed. He was remembering the time he and Alison had first met, and all the emotions that stirred up, and the sight of this young woman moved him deeply.

The two women exchanged some terse comments, the younger one looking to the sky and balling her fists briefly, before shrugging and following her mother out to the street. Harry felt compelled to keep watching, even though he felt like an intruder. The women moved away from him, and once again there was an exchange of words, but this time Anna put her arm around her mother's shoulder, and seemed to steer them both back to their purpose. He did not follow, but turned away to head back to his parked car up the street, with the image of the two women burned into his memory.

The memory would return when, as now sitting in his hotel room in Hamburg, he weighed up in his mind whether he should continue to search for his daughter, introduce himself, attempt to develop a proper relationship with her. He had raised two children, both boys, with his wife. They were now remote and had lives of their own – one now working the North Sea oil rigs as a diver, and the other trading something or other in Hong Kong. He felt a great need to engage with this lost piece of his past. It would occasionally bring waves of regret for words unsaid and actions untaken. Perhaps he was seeking to make amends, or find new meaning in his life. Whatever drove him, he now needed more than ever to meet this young woman.

And yet, here he was having almost found her, and she had disappeared again. But worse he realised he might have put her in harm's way. She was hanging around with a bad guy, who clearly knew some bad people. She seemed to be mixed up in this underworld. Now he felt a new responsibility to protect her, so he needed to find her. But the only lead he had was this man Frank, presumably a gang leader. How else was he going to find a stranger in a strange land? Well, he wasn't without some skills in this kind of work. Only he was a bit rusty.

□

Chapter 21

Potsdam, July 1945

Lieutenant Harry Drayton sat at his desk staring at a piece of paper he was holding in his left hand. In his right hand he held a near identical piece of paper, and he was scanning back and forth between to two, a puzzled look on his face. The door opened abruptly and Captain Dawlish, Harry's immediate commanding officer, strode into the room.

'Drayton,' he said, 'do you have that communique ready for the ambassador?'

'Sir?' Harry looked up distractedly, adjusting to the interruption in his train of thought.

'The intelligence report, Drayton, it has to be with Paris today.'

'Oh yes, sir, it's with the encryption desk now. I had the text approved by that new War Office fellow. You weren't available, but it hadn't changed much since the first draft.'

'Very well, yes that's good. I'm nervous that the ambassador has all the correct intel. We can never trust London to give him all the up-to-date news. God knows how they expect him to do his job and tell them what the French are thinking if they keep blind-siding him. The bloody Russian delegation is up to something and we need to make sure the French are lined up with us and the Americans.'

'I'm not sure De Gaulle would ever get too cosy with the Russians, sir. He's hardly a commie is he?'

'Maybe not, but they have a habit of side-lining us when it comes to the Soviets.'

'The ambassador seems to be holding the fort well. Will he be coming to the conference?'

'I'm still not sure. This bloody election back home is putting everything in doubt. If Attlee wins then it might throw the thing up in the air. And it's beginning to look as if he might.'

'Surely they wouldn't want to change the whole negotiating strategy.'

"Hmm. It's a bloody nuisance all this uncertainty.'

'I thought that's what we've been fighting for – democracy in action. But sir,' Harry quickly changed his tone, leaned forward and waved one of the pieces of paper, 'we may need to be sending another report to the ambassador soon. And not one he'd be pleased to receive, although better he gets it before London.'

'Oh, what's that then?'

Harry laid the two message transcriptions he had been holding on the desk and invited his CO to read them. They were both from a junior attaché to the British embassy in Paris, but each sent to different recipients. One had been sent to London, and the other to their delegation in Germany. Each message was identical except for one detail – the man's expected time of arrival in Potsdam. To London he provided a morning arrival from an overnight train, but to the group in Potsdam he had requested collection from the station late afternoon. Harry had checked the train times, and there were indeed arrivals from Paris at both times.

'So the question is why did he provide different times to different people?' mused Harry.

'How did you get this one? The one for London?'

'I ask for copies of all travel notifications as a matter of course, sir. We've had some mishaps, a few top brass stood at the station for an hour or so. It avoids the headaches.'

'What're your thoughts about this one? Do you think it's significant?'

'He's the new junior liaison with the Russians when the conference starts. My guess is that he's meeting someone, but doesn't want anyone here to know. It may be nothing, but I thought it should be checked. I was about to bring this to you.'

Checks were made, questions were asked, and the sender of the messages was picked up by military intelligence. Soon after Harry heard that the man had been quietly shipped back to England. He never knew the outcome, or whether there had been a serious breach of security, although the Captain did once congratulate him for his excellent vigilance and dedication to duty. A couple of months later he had been approached by counterintelligence to see if he wanted to work for them back in England. At the turn of 1946 he was undergoing an intensive training course for data gathering and analysis, together with techniques for undercover field work – how to ask questions without arousing suspicion. But he found he didn't enjoy it. The war had had a purpose, but this felt like chasing shadows. He wanted to get his former life back.

He had managed to defer his call-up when the war started on the grounds that his new print supply business was helping the war effort. It was ensuring news kept reaching the general population. He was keeping up the morale of the good folk of south Devon. The Devon and Exeter Gazette, he had argued, needed him more than the army. He had been given a few months' grace to find people to keep the business going (his father and a seventeen-year-old driver), but he could not delay it further. His experience in the media world led him into signals. Within a year he had risen to lieutenant responsible for a group running communications out of Southern Command in Salisbury.

As the war progressed methods of communication became more sophisticated, and Harry became involved in transmitting highly classified information, and while he was no crypto-analyst himself, he ran a team with expertise in coding and decoding. It was this work that brought him to the attention of the foreign military attaché service. In October 1944 he was sent to the recently reopened British Embassy in Paris as part of the liaison team with the Allied armies as they advanced on Germany. He would often meet with the ambassador to keep him updated on the latest manoeuvres, enemy actions and, increasingly, the counter-espionage activities that were uncovering the layers of French collaboration that remained. These were gradually being unwoven as the Germans retreated, and Harry played a small role trying to re-normalise international relations. The mission to Potsdam was for him perhaps a crowning achievement. It was the end point of all the effort of the previous six years.

Others around him saw it differently. It was a new beginning. There was a change of government in London, and an emerging idea of a Europe reborn. The mistakes of the past would not be repeated, they said. And there was a new enemy in the Soviet Union, which had emerged from the war more confident, with greater influence and control. There was plenty to be done to keep the country safe.

'Come on, Drayton,' his boss at MI5 had said when he handed in his notice, 'you've been here five minutes, and your training's going very well. We need good men like you.'

'My heart's not in it, sir. I want to get back to Devon and run my business. My father's been holding the fort, but he's not well.'

'We'll be watching you, you know. You've signed the Official Secrets Act, and old Uncle Joe seems to have a long reach.'

'Stalin is of no interest to people in Exeter, sir. They want to know when rationing will end and how they're going to pay the rent. I think there's more to life than chasing spies.'

'Well there's a big task ahead of us here, but doubtless someone has to feed the people their daily diet of news. Good luck, Drayton, perhaps you'll put what you've learned here to good use one day.'

***

Before he left Hamburg, Harry had made one last attempt to contact Frank, with no success. All his enquiries in the bars and clubs he thought the most likely haunts met with him being ignored or misunderstood (feigned or otherwise). In his final encounter there was an aggressive and robust response from a bouncer on a night club door, which clearly indicated that he was getting close, but that it would be unwise to get any closer. Frank and his people would not be the best way to find out where his daughter had gone, and in any case he did not want to risk once again the chance of directing them to the right place to look. However, if he could learn more about their business operations he might get some clues.

He needed to know about this man Frank. If he had a run-in with the police then maybe there would be some public record. The police might be an obvious place to start, but this might alert them to Anna's activities, whatever they were, so he ruled it out. He needed to be cautious. He decided to visit the offices of one of the local newspapers, the Hamburger Abendblatt on Grosser Burstah where he managed to get a few minutes with a reporter from the crime desk. Yes, he was told, there was a local gangland figure named Frank Gottschalg. He had recently been released on bail even though he had been charged with murder. It looked likely that the case against him was about to collapse – a key witness had failed to come forward. The timing of the young couple's disappearance at more or less the same time as Frank's release suggested a strong link, and Harry guessed they would try to get far away, and be as anonymous as possible. He didn't have the resources or the local knowledge to do much more at this point, so he returned to England to work out his next course of action.

Chapter 22

Stories – part 2
London, March 1990

Anna sat agape, staring at her father, unable to take in what she had heard. He waited.

'H-how could you have been there? How could you p-possibly know I was there?' she stammered.

'I was coming to warn you about your nemesis Frank. But it seems he had more to fear than you in the end.'

Anna was silent, but shaking her head and trying to form words. She was beginning to look frightened.

'Anna, we all leave a wake of consequences. We may think we are unimportant or unnoticed. But behind us, around us, people are forever picking over the wreckage of our actions. We have more impact on the world than we think. I followed your trail – once I'd managed to pick it up. What surprised me was that it took so long.'

'Please just tell me how. It sounds like you knew Frank.'

'I'd met him, once. But I learned a lot more about him. I knew he would lead me to you. I wanted to get there first. After you skipped out of Hamburg I guessed he would be pretty upset. He would not have met me personally if he wasn't mad about something, and his type don't ask for apologies. So I paid a local investigator to give me monthly updates on his whereabouts – or more often if he ever left Hamburg. But you had some luck on your side. The police hauled him back into custody for a range of small offences, but not his murder charge. They had him pinned down in Hamburg for the best part of a year. I think he would have found you sooner otherwise.

'There was a trial, a non-custodial sentence, some fines, but he was essentially free again. It probably took him some months to get his business back in order. Get full control of his patch, or whatever these people have to do. But then word came to me that he had aroused the police's attention again. A girl had been beaten up, and her dog killed. It struck me as out of the ordinary. I flew to Hamburg the next day, and went to see her – my contact had given me the details. It turns out she was a friend of yours.'

Anna was beginning to hunch in her seat, with her hand over her mouth. 'Anja – Wolf?' she gasped. She was horrified, and the realisation hit her that she had never given Anja another thought after the shooting.

'Yes, I'm afraid so. I see you didn't know. You never tried to contact her? Another part of your wake. I'm sorry if that sounds harsh, but she was badly beaten. I think she had tried to protect you both, but they killed the dog and threatened that she'd be next. Aaron it seems had made one big error – two actually. The first was that he picked up his criminal activities again, and those drug cartels seem to have lines of communications across the country. The second was that he'd contacted Anja to say how he was getting on in Berlin, and even where he would drink. So once Frank had this much information it wasn't difficult for him to know Aaron's every move in Berlin. He had a couple of days' head start on me, but I hoped he might bide his time before going to Berlin himself. I was on the next train myself.'

'And you happened to be in the same bar at the right time?'

'I went to the district where Anja told me you lived - she didn't have your actual address - and went scouting the bars. I spotted one of Frank's men that I'd met before. He was across the street, coming out of the bar you were in. I saw him beckoning down the street, and there was Frank, with a couple of other men, coming out of another bar. I realised I was too late.'

'What did you see?'

'I got in through the door just as Aaron pulled out his gun. It happened so fast. And you know what happened next.'

'Why didn't you make yourself known to me?'

'You were surrounded by people, they were hustling you out of the back door. Before I knew it you were gone. I knew better than to chase after you.'

'But that was five years ago, what took you so long? Didn't you think I might need some help?'

'It got complicated. The man I knew in Frank's gang – he saw me. He grabbed me and pinned me to a wall. He assumed that I'd already spoken with you, warned you that they were coming. In short, he blamed me for Aaron being armed and ready. He told me that if he ever saw me, or you, again he'd kill both of us. So I left. Came back to England. I felt that if I came back to Germany I'd put you in more danger.'

'That doesn't quite add up. Why didn't this guy come looking for me? I wasn't hiding or anything. I just got on with my life.'

'I don't know. Maybe he was never going back to Berlin, or maybe he got put away – who knows. But it turns out that leaving you alone did no harm. I don't know if it kept you safe, but you're still here. And now I have the chance to put the record straight.'

'What? What do you want to put straight? My dodgy past? Our relationship? What!?'

'I had hoped we might be able to get to know each other. I'd quite like you to think of me as your father. Which, of course, I am.'

She was silent for a while, looking at him then looking away.

'This is beyond weird' she said at last. 'I've known that you are my father for a couple of weeks, and although we have met once before I'm struggling to get my head around this. A complete stranger telling me he had an affair with my mother, who he later abandoned when she probably needed him most. And more than that, some really difficult stuff about my mother's early life that is really upsetting. No wonder she was always so withdrawn and alone. She was on anti-depressants you know? They probably killed her. I wasn't there for her when she needed me. But you weren't there for either of us, ever. I never had a father except a story that was made up.

'You tell me how you have followed me, but you didn't reach out to her in all that time. Didn't you think at least to go and tell her what I was up to?'

Harry's expression changed, and his composure gave way to a look of deep unease. He sat forward, leaning on the table and became more closed in. He was finding it hard to look at her.

'That's rather harsh. I know how it all looks to you, so let me try to defend what appears to be indefensible. Yes, it's true that I let her down, more than once. But my choices were always limited.

'When I first met your mother I was trying to grow a business. That might sound terribly mundane to you, but at the time it was my life. I had a family to support, whom I loved and cherished, and they relied on me completely. Or so I thought. I learned that my wife was seeing someone else, a friend of mine as it happens. I found this out just before I left Exeter for a trip to London, and in the Fitzroy Tavern that night I met this rather lovely woman. Yes, Alison Gardner was attractive, friendly and vulnerable. But at that moment so was I. Something clicked between us. I wasn't planning an affair, but we saw each other each time I came up to town. Like I said, it was intense.

'My wife and I worked through our difficulties – we always did. The children deserved it, we both said. I had always planned to break it off, but Alison never let go. It became fraught, and we argued a lot. I started to see another side to her, one that was troubled and destructive. Self-destructive. I always wondered why she never found a man after the war, how she had remained single all this time. I began to think I knew why. Initially I thought her anger was caused by me not leaving my wife. But she was very hard to love.'

'You never said if you were in love with her.' Said Anna.

'In truth I don't know. I was infatuated, and so was she. When I finally walked away I resolved never to see her again. I was sure that I was bad for her and that we created more harm than harmony. But when my wife died I was at a loose end, and when your past revisits you it becomes very compelling to follow it. Only I couldn't follow it back to her. I knew it would do more damage to both of us.

'But there was you. That was brand new, a real enlightenment. Something good had come from our relationship. It became something of an obsession to find out about you. I never did know how we might meet or what we might say, and the circumstances we find ourselves in are not what I envisaged. But here we are. And I want to make some sort of amends, and I want to get to know you.'

'On what terms? Do you see me as some grateful doting daughter? Or some badge of honour to tell your friends about?'

'No, Anna. I have no expectations, not any more. I was compelled to find you. To let you know of my existence. I have only recently begun to understand how this has invaded your own sense of the past. It must be very destabilising.'

'Most of the last ten years have been unstable for me,' she said, 'but this has been a shocker.'

Anna was not sure how to react. She found the contradictions in his story, her life, and the world beyond impossible to reconcile. This was going to take a while to process. She changed tack.

'Tell me,' she said, 'what do you know about Doug Highcroft? My father – I still think of him as my father. Buy me another gin. It's my turn to tell you a story.'

☐

Chapter 23

Mud and Dust

Saint Laurent-sur-Mer, June 1944

By the evening of 7th June the remnants of GCI 15082 had established a position south east of the village of Saint Laurent-sur-Mer. The camp was basic, and supplies were struggling to arrive. Over the coming days the biggest problem was a lack of drinking water, and trying to get into town to find some was dangerous as the area was surrounded by snipers. The risk was as great that you could get shot by the Americans as by the Germans. The Americans hadn't worked out the difference between the blue-grey of the RAF and the iron grey of the German uniforms. There were rumours that several of the RAF casualties were due to friendly fire on D-Day, although no-one knew the specifics.

Richard Hurrell put his head into Fordham's tent on the third evening. 'Hello, Padre. Just thought I'd pop in to say hello. See how you are.'

'I'm fine, thanks - how are you?'

'Between the damp and the dust I suppose I'm skipping along. In truth there's not much to do since we shipped out the last of the serious casualties. It's all very tedious.'

'Whereas I've been too busy. They've been burying the dead up on the hill the other side of town, so my presence is somewhat in demand. I'm planning a service for the fallen in a few weeks' time, when we know we have accounted for everyone.'

'I think I'd like to go up there soon, pay my respects. You know I'm still a little haunted by Duggie, wondering what we could have done differently.'

'Don't be doing that. It was an 88mm that killed him. It could have been any of you. What little I learned of the man he was the life and soul.'

'I'm still wearing his jumper - look. In fact I also have his kit bag in my tent. I rescued this.' He held up a flask of gin. 'He was well-provisioned anyway. I feel terribly guilty at the thought of drinking it though.'

'I suggest you take that bottle round to Jerry Mays and have a drink together. I think he could do with the respite - he's been working flat out to get the new equipment up and running. He may not have had much time to grieve for his friend.'

'Good idea. I'll do that.'

'Any news of Vince Reedbanks?'

'He was shipped out the next day. He was a bit delirious from the morphine the last time I saw him. He kept telling me to thank Doug for saving his life. I'd say he's going to struggle with this.'

They agreed to go up to the cemetery together when the ground was dryer and the burials were complete.

Hurrell found Jerry coming out of the makeshift Ops tent. There was the constant thrumming of the diesel generator, and for the first time Hurrell noticed that the arial had been assembled. 'It's not connected to anything yet,' said Jerry, 'we're still waiting for some serviceable receiver stations. It'll be another day or so before we're up and running. But at least we have power now.'

Hurrell held up the flask of gin. 'You look like you could do with some of this,' he said, 'have you got some time to take it easy?'

'Well there's not much more I can do here until the kit arrives. Frankly I could do with a stiff drink.'

They went to Jerry's tent where he found a couple of mugs. 'Cheers!' they said as the clunked the tin cups together.

'You look all in.'

'Hardly slept,' said Jerry, 'been working like hell to salvage some of the equipment. Most if it was drowned. Anything that made it to shore either took a direct hit or was abandoned to the incoming tide. Astonishingly they got us a replacement antenna from England yesterday. I hear 15083 up at Juno are fully operational. So at least we have some air cover now. You must have had a busy time.'

'It was full on for the first two days, but most of the casualties have been shipped out, so in truth I've been at a bit of a loose end all day. I'm worried that these snipers are going to keep us busy though. I don't know what's worse, the boredom or the horror.'

'Take the boredom old man. With any luck the main show will be moving away from us, so we won't see too much direct combat.'

'Duggie was a friend of yours wasn't he? I'm sorry there was nothing we could do.'

'Yes, we'd worked together on and off since last summer. Me, Doug and Vince had been posted together to start training teams for this kind of operation. We had no idea it would be like this though. Now there's only me left. How was Vince when you last saw him? I never got a chance to see him'

'He was heavily sedated. He's got a long road to recovery ahead of him, but prosthetics are getting better all the time, so he'll be able to function again, but no more active duty for him.'

'I haven't had much time to think about Doug. It's probably why I've thrown myself into building the station, even if we don't have all the bits left. Keeping busy is important. You know what concerns me most?'

'What's that?'

'Telling his fiancée. Well, she wasn't officially his fiancée, but Doug told me they were planning to marry after the war. I knew her a little. Lovely girl. She'll be devastated.'

'But it won't be up to you to tell her.'

'No, but I'm sure she'll be in touch at some point. She will want to know what happened. I won't know what to say.'

'Tell her the truth. Do you think she could cope with it.'

'I should say so. I don't think she'd stand for anything less.' Jerry paused before carrying on. 'You know, this may be the gin talking, but it strikes me that we are living through something we'll never forget. It's going to be with us for the rest of our lives. I know it has changed me, all this death and mayhem I've seen. And if we win this thing, if we make sure no-one has to do this again, our children won't know what it's like. We'll be protecting them from the horror, but stealing from them this shared purpose. If it's not about lasting peace what's it all going to be for?'

'There's a big question. It was Duggie - Doug - who impressed on me the importance of what we were about to do. I'm grateful to him for that. It made the events on that beach more urgent than ever.'

***

Ten days later Richard Hurrell and the Padre borrowed a couple of bicycles and rode over to the cemetery. The ground was still churned and rough, but the graves had been set out in neat rows. There were white crosses being placed on each of them, with names and numbers hand written on them. A more permanent solution would be installed when there was more time to devote to the dead.

'We are planning a service for them next week. The crosses should be in place by then. I doubt this will be their final resting place. My guess is they will be moved later. Come on this way, the RAF has the corner down there.'

After a few minutes searching they located Doug Highcroft's grave, his name hastily written on the cross. They also recognised the names of other colleagues in the adjacent graves. They stood in silence for a while.

'It's funny,' said the Padre, 'we are both used to seeing people at each side of life's great divide. I don't know about you, but I still can't fathom how the sense of loss grips us completely. Nothing prepares you for it, and each time it is different. The passing of a unique spirit.'

'As a medic I think we get a bit blasé about death. Until it's someone we know. But, yes, I agree. Each one is unique. But this is different for me. Such carnage is beyond what I imagined. We heard stories in medical school about the Great War, but it seemed so remote.

Tell me, Padre, do you think every generation is destined to go through this?'

'There have always been wars, Richard, but this one is even bigger than the last. If you ask me we need to find a way to make sure this doesn't happen again. It would be nice if we could give our children a better world.'

'Yes. Jerry said something similar. I think.'

***

Exactly one year to the day after D-Day, Jerry Mays finally put pen to paper. He was replying to Eleanor's letter asking him what happened on that beach. She had been told that he was next to Doug when it happened. He had been putting off writing this letter for at least two months. He kept telling himself he was too busy, seeing out the end of the war. But he knew this was a lame excuse, and spurred on by the date - 6 June 1945 - he realised he couldn't delay it any further.

After writing a direct and frank account of what he had witnessed he was left in no doubt that she needed to know the fate of the man she loved. He didn't know if he would ever see her again. He thought it unlikely. He ended the letter with the following paragraph:

'I went to the funeral service which was held about three weeks later over the graves of our fellows and many others besides. But it was held for our fellows by our Padre. It was a beautiful day. As we stood on the hill this eye followed the lines of white crosses to the sea. The balloons shone silver against the blue sky and white clouds floated over. It was very quiet here – the Hun had been driven many miles inland. And before us lay the price.'

Chapter 24

Fitzroy Tavern
London, December 1958

On days like this the city was dreary grey, the buildings merging into the sky, with everything seemingly bleached by the cold wind. It blew from the east and Goodge Street funnelled it into a constant stream, cold and bone dry, stark and severe. Eleanor found herself pushed along by the breeze, as she hurried to get away from its menace. She wished even more that she was back at home with the two children, just two and three years old and left in the care of their aging nanny. And now carrying another inside her, she suddenly felt a deep guilt that she should not be here, back in her old haunts. She had been so looking forward to this trip, had been longing to get back to touch her old life and reconnect with the city she knew so well and loved so much. But the wind, the cold, the separation from her children made it seem so pointless and bleak. But she promised she would come, and of course she was looking forward to dinner later at the White Tower with her husband, Robert.

What would it be like walking into the print works and seeing all those faces? She had not seen any of her former colleagues since the wedding, since she started what had soon felt like an enforced seclusion. Imprisonment almost. She didn't dare think these words. They seemed like an act of disloyalty, treachery almost. Robert had been so good to her, and he seemed to adore her, in his own way. But the suburban house in a dormitory town, a full fifty minute train ride from the city, felt remote, lonely and oppressive. The children had changed that, and she learned to build a household and gradually found the confidence to make it her own. She started to find a vision for it, and build some hopes and dreams. She often reflected that this was not what she expected from life, but then her generation were thrown into the biggest uncertainty of all. When they emerged from the ruins of the war they looked around to pick up where they could and start the whole thing afresh. In her case that was exactly what she felt. Allow the past to fold gently over itself into obscurity, and plough on into a future that she could learn to trust.

As Eleanor turned the corner into Charlotte Street the wind abruptly abated and her anxiety dropped a little with it. She wasn't sure why she had agreed to this meeting, apart from an excuse to make a trip to London, and she was apprehensive. She was out of practice at walking into pubs on her own, of meeting people she barely knew, and having adult conversations with anyone but her husband or the nanny. It had once been so natural for her. She smiled at the times she would wait at the bar of the Dog and Duck for 'the late Mr Roe' as Robert would frame it. Mr Roe was always the last one to shut up the office in the evening.

She stepped through the door of the Fitzroy Tavern into the snug and at a small table sat Alison Gardner, whom she'd last seen a few years before standing behind that very bar. Eleanor moved briskly to the table, removing her gloves and hat, and remembering to smile.

'Hello,' she said, 'I hope I'm not too late. The train seemed to stop for ages outside St Pancras Station.'

'No that's fine,' said Alison, 'I've not been here long myself. Thank you ever so much for seeing me.'

And now Eleanor could see that Alison was heavily pregnant, but looked ashen and worn down.

'I'm sorry I had no idea, congratulations! I would have brought you a little something if I had known. I had no idea you were married.'

'Oh don't worry, you wouldn't have known. Let me get you a drink. A sandwich perhaps?'

'I'll have a tonic water please. I'm actually expecting myself – just 3 months. Can't bear the taste of gin at the moment! But I am a bit peckish. Let me give you some money.'

'Congratulations to you! Well, well, we're both in the same boat. I hope not exactly the same boat.' There was an exchange of curious glances. Eleanor tilted her head and raised an eyebrow as Alison, eyes widening and a tight-lipped smile, got up and moved towards the bar. 'And please, this is on me. I get a few perks here as a member of staff.'

Eleanor looked around her. This place used to be so familiar. She tried to avoid the hustle and bustle of the public bar, but she always enjoyed the vibrancy, the ever-presence of the landlady, and the cast of characters that came and went. She started to feel more relaxed and more in tune with her surroundings. Alison returned with the drinks. Eleanor noted the half pint of bitter she had bought herself and found herself wincing a little. In her experience women and beer didn't sit well together, but that was another story, and one she wasn't going to discuss today.

Alison offered a cigarette, which Eleanor declined.

'I'm trying to give up. I'm not comfortable smoking in the house with two little ones. And besides they're now saying we shouldn't smoke while pregnant. I'm not sure about all that though.'

'No,' said Alison, 'I don't know what that's about. I don't have many pleasures, and the odd one can't hurt, can it?' She lit up.

'So do tell me why you wanted to meet me so much? We hardly knew each other back at Langtoft. There was nothing really that we had in common.'

'Except for Doug, but I'll come to that. I saw the wedding photo in the paper. I recognised your husband first. He used to come in here quite a lot, and then there was that time you were with him. I could see something was going on.'

'I was his secretary, there was nothing going on.'

'Oh please! I've worked behind bars long enough to notice what the punters are up to. But that's not my business. I'm certainly no-one to judge. But since seeing the picture you've been in the back of my mind. I realised I needed to talk to someone about the past, the war. I never made any lasting friends – especially not over in Norfolk – it all rather fell apart for me.'

'Couldn't you go home?'

'No I could never have done that. And anyway my life got a bit complicated.' Alison recounted the story of Harry and his sporadic appearances, his failures to support her, especially over the miscarriage.

'And now here I am again. Kid on the way, lousy man hardly in my life, dead-end job. What I want to know is how did you pick yourself up? After Doug was killed. I never thought about it much at the time. Men died all the time, never came back from the war. But losing that baby before, well that was the first time I'd really lost anyone, and it floored me. Yes, both my parents died, but I promise you that was no loss.'

'Well, Alison, dear, I'm sorry you're in such a bad way, but I still don't understand where I fit in to all this.'

'No. No you wouldn't, I suppose. It's all in my head. Listen, I'm going to leave Harry – he won't even know I've left him, I'll disappear and he won't be able to find me. But I'm going to need a father for this child. This one's going to be a survivor, I know it. And he or she is going to need a good father figure to look up to. And let's face it, look at me – I'm spent. I'll never find a decent man now.'

'That's nonsense. Never say never.'

'I haven't the energy for it – a new relationship, fear of rejection, looking for the signs of a cheating heart. But I know I can bring up this child, and I want them to believe they had a good father. One that cared about people, one that had some courage and adventure. I know if I believe it myself, they'll feel it too. So what I wanted to ask of you, Eleanor – I want to ask you to give me Doug.'

'What? I don't understand you.'

'I want to take his name. Build a story, and make him live. At least survive the Normandy beaches. If he had, then that child in you right now could have been his. He took his love for you to the grave, but I'm sure you carry some of him around with you still. So I need to ask your permission. It would honestly feel like theft if I didn't. It's a simple thing that I ask, but I know it comes with a cost.'

When Eleanor left the Fitzroy Tavern and headed for Foley Street she felt like she had walked into a new world. She had thought that she had put the past behind her. She was married to a man who had pulled her into his life. She was well-provided for, and had moved in West End circles she had only gazed at from a distance in the past. And she had children – which she had begun to give up hoping for. She sometimes worried about the age difference between herself and her husband, and she found herself lonely in their dormitory town especially with the long work hours her husband kept. The house they lived in was full of ghosts of his first marriage – unhappy and wrecked by alcohol. But she counted herself as one of the lucky ones to have stability, security and comfort through the never-ending austerity of rationing. The children had made this complete.

Now she felt a chill wind cut through her as she was flung back into her past loss and longing. Doug had died, their future denied them by the indifferent brutality of war, and she had been determined to get on and build a life. Being singled out and flattered by her boss – hand-picked from the typing pool of a customer – she had found a way to give her life new purpose. But the costs had been high, and it seemed she was now to be forced to relive her pain and anguish of losing Doug once more. She wasn't going to deny Alison her request, but she couldn't provide her unconditional blessing either. She knew there was nothing she could do about it, and Alison was in greater need of her own touchstone and anchor if she was to raise a child on her own. Eleanor did what she always did – she drew in tight, as if she was pulling the blood flow from her extremities back to her core. Outwardly she said all the right words, even smiled as she spoke them, but inwardly she promised herself she would never release Doug from her heart.

In that short walk to the print works she found herself filled with contradictions. The child inside her with the promise and hope for the future (that years later the precariousness of the Cuban missile crisis would rob from her); the walking back into her old workplace and faces left behind when she traded being the boss's secretary for being his wife; and the surreal world of her lost love and an invention for him to have new life. Alison's unborn child to be raised with a fictional father, a man she had once dreamed would be her own future.

Eleanor vividly recalled the Christmas Eve in that farmhouse on the edge of the Fens when Doug had proposed. She remembered his broad smile when she said yes, his eyes glittering in the firelight when he told her:

'Darling, it will be wonderful. Our lives will be wonderful, I promise. Just imagine what our children will be like.'

She felt a stirring from the little life growing inside her.

☐

Chapter 25

Portland Bill, April 1990

On a bright April morning, Anna sat in the kitchen of her mother's house - her house - with the urn containing her mother's ashes on the table in front of her. In a moment of lucidity a couple of days before she had understood what she wanted to do. Now, as she sat leaning back in her chair, legs stretched out in front of her and staring at the urn, her two friends moved silently around her, making coffee, scratching at pieces of toast. The three of them had driven down the previous afternoon. A rowdy drive that had included a stop at Stonehenge to wander among the stones - Molly had never been before, and Jane wanted to reprise her childhood memories of sitting on one of the fallen lintels. The evening had been reflective as Anna related everything she understood about her past. They planned to set out early the next day.

They drove up through Exeter before taking the road down to Lyme Regis, hugging the Dorset coast. They chit-chatted about the lovely Dorset villages they drove through, and wondered at the various monuments and ruins they passed on the way. They had regular views of Chesil Beach, that long spit that connects the English mainland with the Isle of Portland. Anna recalled going there once with her mother. The pair of them had set out walking from Hive beach with the intent of getting as far as they could, but found themselves exhausted from the loose shingle and turned back after realising it was a never-ending quest. Their search for fossils in the Jurassic clay did not yield anything more than a soft ammonite that crumbled as they moved it from its ancient resting place. Anna wondered why she had never come back to this place with its stark, wild beauty.

As the car journey progressed the scenery changed, and Anna found herself becoming more uncomfortable. They were driving through the outskirts of Weymouth when she started wondering whether she was doing the right thing. These streets looked like any other town in England, and the day was turning overcast removing any sparkle or light they might possess. When they crossed the short bridge onto Portland, with the last views of the south end of Chesil Beach, Anna was feeling fully miserable and was ready to tell Molly to turn the car around. But she stayed silent. After they wound their way through the last of the urban areas, the land and sea opened up before them. It was flat and bleak, but Anna felt something stirring in her, something that told her this might be the right place. The road ended in front of the large red and white lighthouse at what felt like the end of England.

By midday, Anna stood at the tip of Portland Bill next to the Trinity House Obelisk. She noted the date that it was erected, 1844, exactly one hundred years before Doug Highcroft died on a Normandy beach. Looking out over the English Channel she finally understood that all life is contingent. Nothing is a given, and nothing necessarily follows from anything else; any choices we make do not lead to where we want to go. All connections are ephemeral and become lost in the tangle of time. But now she was reconnecting them to see how the pathways of her buried past had brought her to this point and they formed a web, not a line.

Although she never had a sense of direction when she was young, she was convinced that leaving home would reveal a plan. On would come a light and there it would be, her golden future exposed at last. The world that had been mysteriously going on without her when she was a teenager would suddenly pull her into its flow. She would be inducted into its secrets, the mystery revealed. It certainly did pull her in (and under), but now she knew there was no plan, no big secret, one figured out what to do next as events happened. Looking into the future is like looking into a mist where details blur and disappear, and now she was learning to be comfortable with that.

A lone sailing dinghy moved across her line of sight. She imagined it caught in a squall, getting into trouble and overturning. Who can say when a life ends? And who knows the impact of a life lost? We are told stories that mean nothing to us, until we become part of them. Then we know what the storyteller was trying to say, a need to pass on a little of themselves, to be understood. Even if the story was a fabrication, a lie, it still held a truth that the teller wanted to reveal. Doug died here in her mother's telling - only he didn't. But he undoubtedly knew this place and this coast. The light from this beacon would have been one of his last sights of England as he sailed to his demise. And Alison also knew this spot. Perhaps she had stood here wondering what to tell her unborn child. Perhaps every time she recounted the story to the child she pictured this view in her mind's eye, or at least a wilder version of it. A torn sail and overturned hull being thrown around by a suddenly angry sea.

Doug must have meant something special to Alison, why else would she adopt him to be her child's father, to give her his name? Whatever their relationship, though, she would have been disappointed. He was in love with someone else, possibly never gave her much of a thought. Anna wondered about that other woman, and the grief she must have endured. What was her story? What of her family? She considered trying to find her, after all she had a name. Her friendly lord of the realm might know where she was. Howard said he had met her children. He had shown them around the Houses of Parliament one time. Her own story had nothing to do with that person, and to connect with her could only stir up more grief and trouble. It wouldn't be fair. Anna was having a hard enough time coming to terms with her own reality to transfer the burden of her life of ghosts to another unwitting soul.

Her real father was a self-confessed ghost, with no substance or form; something caught fleetingly and quickly dispersed. One that seemed to vanish every time she needed him most. Whereas a real ghost, a full-on haunting that inhabited her synaptically, if not genetically, was the father that gave her meaning and hope. Maybe her mother had given her a proper father after all, even though he was just a story. A real man who had in some way touched Alison's life, and that she felt more worthy of being a father to her child than the philanderer who had abandoned her. Alison's depression probably exacerbated her insecurities and it would not be surprising for her to seek out some solidity in her life, there was something rooted about the tragic loss of a good man. A dead hero cannot let you down, and the story you create about him can be crafted to meet your own needs.

What of the man, Doug? Was he a hero, or a hapless victim? How to judge? She did not know. But she knew this: he died, aged almost 26, believing he was fighting for a better world. She didn't buy all the jingoistic sentiment around 'plucky little Blighty', but she recognised that his generation were prepared to give up everything so that her life would be better – a life of choices. It was co-operation between people and nations that won out; dogma and nationalism lost. She found herself wondering about the young gunner who had killed Doug. Whether he was still alive, and if so whether he hung on to his youthful ideals. She had learned that the nation she called home for eight years, one that had been a mortal enemy less than fifty years before, was alive, vibrant, creative and welcoming. But it still contained dark shadows of its past, and she also found these reflected in her native England. The fight was never won, it just moved on. She resolved at that moment that any child of hers would understand this. She knew these lessons must not be lost. And what came next was as much for Doug as for her mother.

The tide was high. Anna left the stone circle around the obelisk and walked to the cliff edge to her left. While the cliffs were not particularly high she still got an uneasy sense of vertigo as she peered over. There was a faint offshore breeze, and the waves below gently washed over the rocks. As a teenager she had enjoyed contemplating the movement of the waves on a shore; it held an eternal mystery, yet was constant and persistent. You could rely on the uncertainty of the sea. She glanced towards the lighthouse where her friends were waiting. They waved. She waved back. She turned to the cliff edge and removed the lid from the urn. In one easy move she stretched out her arms, tipping the vessel at full reach, with the contents spilling in a smooth and steady flow onto the waters below. The ashes seemed to dance on the surface as they were swirled around, until some laps of surf folded them into the body of the waves, to be forever restless within the currents and tides of the open sea beyond.

☐

Epilogue

Dear Anja,

I hope this letter reaches you, as I do not have an up-to-date address for you. If you have moved then I'm relying on this being forwarded somehow.

Firstly I want to apologise for not being in touch sooner. I only recently learned what happened to you at the hands of that group of murderous thugs. It must have been devastating for you. Contacting you now cannot make up for my complete thoughtlessness and selfishness, but it's the best I can do. I can't offer any real explanation for my actions – or rather inactions – other than I think I tried to block out everything from Aaron's world. I had to remake myself, so I focussed on the here and now and never looked back.

But Anja, you saved my life, and then you paid the price for my stupidity, while I was completely ignorant of the damage I had done. I want you to know that I am deeply sorry for that. And for little Wolf. You loved that dog, and to have him taken from you like that must have been horrible in the extreme.

As you can see from the postmark I am now back in England. After Aaron was put away I stayed on in Berlin and finished my engineering degree. I had a good job in the end, but I ran out of steam and something kept pulling me home. But it all got a bit weird here over the past few months. I lost my mother before I could reconcile with her, and met my father who I never knew existed. This was Harry who came to see you. I don't know if he told you who he was, but he told me about you. It made me realise how completely rubbish I have been. It was a very low point for me.

So, Anja, it seems I am not the person I thought I was – in so many ways. I got my parents wrong – by deception or ignorance –, got my boyfriend all wrong, and completely abandoned any friends I ever had. I don't quite know the way back, or where 'back' even is. I only hope that you can forgive me. If I don't hear back from you then it might be a sign that you don't want to *know me. But until I know that for certain I won't give up trying to contact you. Right now I think my life is about not giving up.*

Your grateful and loving friend
Anna

☐

Author's Note

   This book was born out of a desire to connect with the ambiguities of the past. Some of the action from the Second World War is loosely based on real events which have been pieced together from my own family records, and other archives that are in the public domain. I am particularly grateful to the keepers of the website 'The Royal Air Force at Omaha Beach', which is a tremendous archive and testimony to the events of June 1944. All the characters are fictionalised, but some of the central characters and their relationships are an imagined telling of what I believe might have occurred in real life. Without going into detail, suffice to say that if the events on Omaha Beach had taken a different turn, this book would not have been written. This book is dedicated to all those who have been unable to tell their stories due to their own selfless sacrifice.

Acknowledgement

I would like to thank everyone who has contributed to the making of this book. In particular my family and friends who read early drafts and provided valuable feedback and advice. Elaine and Jon Dean, Paul Brown, my brother and sister-in-law, Richard and Fiona. Many thanks to my editors, Martin Fletcher and Tim Pedley for their excellent professional input, and to Martin Lore for the cover artwork. A huge thanks to my wife Kathy who supported the venture all the way. And finally to my late mother, without whom this tale would not have been told.☐

Printed in Great Britain
by Amazon